THE AUSTRALIAN BILLIONAIRE

A CLEAN, INTERNATIONAL BILLIONAIRE CLUB ROMANCE

BRITNEY M MILLS

CRYSTAL CANYON PRESS

To Bree Livingston

*For giving me the courage to write this book and for always being there when
I need inspiration or instruction.*

Jackson Walker ran a hand through his hair, trying to make sense of the end of year numbers the accountant had given him that morning. January was not his favorite time of year as it neared time for his birthday once again. He'd come so far from the small island of Tasmania, but even though he'd be turning thirty in a few weeks, sometimes the memories of his childhood still crept in. That's when the idea that he was a billionaire seemed like a dream, as if he'd wake up at any moment and be scraping by.

He'd never met his father, and his mother hadn't been ready to take care of a child. After a few years of bouncing among family members, he'd been put into the foster care system. For years, he'd hoped each foster family would surprise him with an adoption, but after a while, he realized he was just biding time in each home until another one became available. He'd see the kids at the park with two loving parents and wonder why he couldn't have the same thing.

And now he was too busy to consider having a family, or even start by finding the right woman. He thought that having money would be the ultimate success of his life, proving to many that he'd been able to make something out of nothing. But when it came to people, especially women, he found they were more attracted to his wealth than his personality.

Rubbing at his eyes, he focused on the numbers again, hoping to sort them all out in his mind. He was a people person, able to negotiate with some of the most difficult people and end up friends with them later, but numbers always took longer to sink in.

The previous year had been successful for CC Sporting Goods, the shop he owned in downtown Sydney. It had been open for five years, along with a sister store in Brisbane still thriving after three years.

A text dinged from his phone and he turned it over, grinning to see it was one of his good friends and frat brothers, Roman Hamilton.

Just went to the sporting goods store here in London. It was pitiful. Any chance CC Sports is going to have a store here soon?

When you find me some property that won't make me choke when I look at the price, mate.

It took a few minutes for the response to come in, but the answer sounded just like Roman.

I'm on it. I'll shoot you some options later.

Jackson put down his phone, shaking his head. He'd been good friends with a number of his frat brothers, and they'd all become relatively successful in their fields. Roman was in real estate development and Jackson didn't doubt he'd see several commercial properties end up in his inbox later.

Shaking his head, he pushed the papers to the corner of his desk. He'd have to go over them another time when his mind cleared. Sitting back, he stretched, focusing completely on the trip he'd been planning to California, now only two weeks away. Home of his college alma mater, it had been two years since his last trip to visit, and he missed it. He'd always held the unspoken desire to open a store there, in commemoration of starting a new life and of the man who'd helped that happen.

Coach Dan Montgomery had been instrumental in giving Jackson a new perspective on life, helping him to see that even the littlest mistakes made in fun could be life-changing. He'd arrived in Anaheim

Hills as a naïve teenager who thought the world owed him something, and he'd left a man, ready to take on his future.

He'd attended Hawthorne University, graduating eight years ago. He'd kept in touch with his coach, as well as several of his fraternity brothers, meeting up with them as often as he could, but with the distance between them all, it made it difficult for more than weekly or monthly calls.

It wasn't as if he didn't have the money to visit frequently. Now, anyway. It was the work that kept him busy in Australia, the constant research. With managers and employees to run his stores, it had really become about maintenance and keeping on top of their training. The rest of his time was spent researching and working to come up with cutting edge technology or products everyday people and athletes could use.

The first thing he'd invented was a new type of headset for football coaches to communicate with the other coaches and players during games. They were all digital, waterproof, and closed-circuit, meaning the interruptions were significantly less than before. The NFL and NCAA used the headsets exclusively, as did many other sports organizations. The exclusivity brought in the bulk of his wealth, so staying on top of any changes and progress came before anything else.

The inspiration had come from Coach Montgomery. Jackson smiled as he remembered Coach griping about overhearing the radio when he was trying to communicate to the coaches in the upper box one game during Jackson's sophomore year of college. When Jackson had come to him with the idea shortly after graduation, Coach had done all he could to connect him to the right people, from the research to production. His wife had accepted him into their home each time he'd visited over the years, and it was there that Jackson truly felt like he was home.

A knock came at the door, pulling him from his thoughts. He looked up to see his secretary peeking in. "There's a call for you, Mr. Walker. It's from the States."

"Send it through, Heidi." He gave her a quick smile, and she nodded, shutting the door again. A red light blinked on his phone, and he heard the ring.

Picking it up, he said, "G'day, this is Jackson."

A sniffle sounded from the other line, and something clenched his lungs. "Jackson." The voice was familiar, but one word didn't help him place it.

"This is Jackson. How may I help you?"

"I'm sorry. This is Cari Montgomery." She paused again, and his mind raced. Coach's wife? Did something happen to Coach?

"Mrs. M., what's wrong?" He looked all over his office, as if that would help him figure out why she was sobbing.

Mrs. Montgomery took in a deep breath and said, "I'm sorry to tell you over the phone, but Dan passed away a few hours ago."

Jackson's mouth dropped open, the words a jumbled mess in his mind. "Coach? What happened? Why?" He felt a sharp pain slice through his chest. He'd loved the guy like a father.

"He had stage four liver cancer. There was nothing they could do." She sniffed again, and Jackson's vision blurred.

"He didn't drink." He didn't know it was possible to get liver cancer without being a complete drunk. He'd heard his biological grandfather had died of liver cancer, but that had been when the man was older, and after at least a decade void of sobriety.

Resting his forehead on the desk, Jackson worked to breathe in, holding it a few seconds before breathing out.

"Sometimes it just happens."

A tear broke free, its coolness feeling odd against his burning skin. "When—when is the funeral?"

Another pause caused Jackson's thoughts to swirl, memories of Coach Montgomery parading around. Happier times.

"On Wednesday, here in California. Is there some way you can make it—"

"I'll get on a flight as soon as I can." He pulled out his calendar, knowing he'd have to arrange his schedule to accommodate this.

"Will you contact the others from the IBC?"

Mrs. M.'s use of the nickname her husband had given him and his frat brothers back in the day made him smile. They'd started out as the Trying Ten when Dan Montgomery became the house mentor for Delta Phi. But by the time they were seniors, he'd changed it to the Top-Notch Ten, or TNT for short.

Just a few years ago, they'd all managed to get together in France for a marketing conference Tristan, one of his frat brothers had put on. Since Tristan represented each of their businesses in marketing, it had been the perfect opportunity to meet up. When they'd figured out all ten were billionaires, they'd made up the International Billionaire Club as a joke, or IBC for short. But it had stuck, and people close to them used it to avoid having to list all of the guys.

Clicking through a mental list of the guys, he said, "Yes, I'll let them know before I leave for the airport. Some of them will have to fly out soon to make it in time."

"Thank you." Her voice was little more than a whisper. "I wish we could wait a bit longer, but family schedules make that hard to do. You'll make it, right?"

Jackson frowned. Had she not heard him the first time? "I wouldn't miss it for anything."

"It'll be good to see you. I just wish it wasn't under these circum-stances. Please let me know when you get into town. You'll stay at the house?"

"Uh," he said, unsure what to say. "You sure you have room? With everyone coming for the funeral, I don't want to intrude."

A light laugh floated through the line, and he was grateful for that at least. "Jackson, you're family. You're always welcome to stay with us."

His lips trembled, and he wiped at the tears that flowed freely now, the words 'you're family' hitting him harder than he'd expected. "Thank you." His voice cracked on the last part. He waited a moment, hoping to control the tidal wave, before he said, "See you soon, Mrs. M."

He hung up the phone, not wanting her to hear more as he couldn't hold back the emotions any longer. Slipping out of his chair and onto the floor, he pulled his knees in tight and sobbed. He was grateful no one walked in during that time because it wasn't something he wanted to explain.

Several minutes passed until he couldn't cry anymore; even then a large chasm remained in his chest. Sitting back in his seat, he picked up the phone receiver.

"Heidi?"

"Yes, sir?"

"I need to book the next flight to California." He pulled a tissue from a box on his desk and held the phone away from his ear, blowing his nose.

"What about your big meeting tomorrow?" she asked. Jackson could hear her clicking and moving things around on her desk.

"I'll have to join it as a conference call. This takes precedence."

CHAPTER 2

Tuesday could not go any slower for Hailey Montgomery. She was working through an internal debate about whether or not she should be at home with her mother and siblings. Part of her knew that if she stopped working and thought about her father's passing, it would take weeks to pick herself back up again. Guilt propelled the nagging feeling to flow throughout her, and she picked up several files from her desk, needing to spread them out on a larger surface to concentrate on the listings.

Sitting down at a conference table, her thoughts turned to her mother, who was doing her best to get through this first full day without her husband in more than thirty-five years. Focusing on her work, Hailey laid out the files in order of where they were located in the area. As a real estate agent in Southern California, she did a lot of research for her potential and current clients. When she found something they liked, it always filled her with a motivation to give them the world, within their budget. She was lacking that motivation today.

As much as she wanted to mourn the loss of her father, she was still furious at the fact that he hadn't wanted his children to know about his illness until the week before he died. She hadn't had enough time to process it all, and she'd never found the chance to really thank him for everything he'd done for her, especially in the past eight years.

"Hailey, what are you doing here?" She could hear the surprise in Jonathan's voice, but she wasn't in the mood for pity or a lecture as to why she was working. Her boss was rarely in the office, but he *would* pick today to come in.

"I'm trying to stay afloat. I had several people call about properties yesterday, and we're closing on the Farnsworth property this after-noon." She sat back in the seat, giving him a small smile.

He frowned at her, his lips pursed, and she had to look away. That small action reminded her of her father. He'd do that when he wasn't happy about a current choice in her life. Not that she'd done bad things, but times like when she'd decided to go into real estate instead of nursing or social work. Or when she'd stopped speaking to him about football.

"We can have someone cover that until you get back. Shouldn't you be with your family right now?"

The guilt she'd felt earlier ripped through her chest. She should. She should be comforting her mother and her younger brother and sister. But that would make the reality of the situation more real than she wanted it to be. Her mother, the traitor who'd kept her father's illness a secret for months.

She shook her head. "What I need to do is keep working to take my mind off it."

Jonathan leaned forward, resting his hands on the glass conference table, his brows furrowed. "No. What you need to do is take some time off work. I'll make sure your accounts are taken care of and that the signing for the Farnsworth house goes through this afternoon. If there's anything big, I'll make sure to call and ask about it. But as of right now, you're on a mandatory two-week vacation."

Hailey's mouth dropped open. "You can't do that."

"I'm the boss. Your father just passed away yesterday. Take some time. Grieve. You've been working more than ever lately, and it shows. I just don't want you to burn out."

Wrapping her arms around her middle, Hailey felt the start of a burning sensation in her nose, her eyes ready to fill with tears at her command. She tamped down her emotions, determined not to feel. She looked up at her boss, ready to debate, but gave up when she saw he wasn't going to back down.

Throwing the papers back into her files, she said, "Let me get everything I have, and then I'll go home. You promise you'll call, though, right? You won't make any big decisions on my accounts without me?"

Jonathan raised his hand in the air. "I promise I will call you first before anything major happens."

She took a deep breath and left the conference room. As much as she didn't want to be at her childhood home right now, she wanted to be in her silent apartment even less. It was too quiet, reminding her of the milestones she hadn't reached yet at twenty-nine years old.

Her last real relationship ended nearly five years earlier and after all the trust she'd put into her baseball ex, his betrayal hurt more than anything, making it difficult to trust again. Men with money acted like they could do no wrong, or if they threw enough money at something, it would just go away.

She had to laugh as she thought of her last date, someone her aunt Sarah had lined up for her two months ago. They'd gone to a pizza place, and he'd told her all about what he'd name their future children and what month would be best for a wedding. With the right guy those topics would be exciting, but never on a first date.

Not that she was that great at choosing for herself either. The handful of other dates had seemed normal when they'd first met, but after the first or second date, they felt comfortable to share their darkest secrets, not usually things she wanted to put up with more than an hour, let alone a lifetime.

She'd thought she'd hit the boyfriend jackpot once. Avery had been her boyfriend the year after graduating with her bachelor's, and things had been progressing to the point that she was waiting for a ring. He'd played third base for his time at Hawthorne, graduating a few years before she went there. He was also the first athlete she'd dated since she'd decided athletes were just overcompensated babies who couldn't do anything for themselves.

Memories of those days still haunted her, and she shivered as she pushed the thoughts away. After packing up a few things, she dropped all her current client files off on Jonathan's desk and waved to Cindy, the company secretary, on the way out.

"I'm so sorry to hear about your father," she called after Hailey.

When Hailey made it to the elevator, she turned and gave the woman a half-smile. Under her breath she said, "Me too. Me too."

* * *

PULLING into the driveway of her parents' property, Hailey parked to the side of the house. It was her brother's spot now that she had moved out, but his car was gone. She thought about Junior and was surprised to find her heart ached more than it already did. Each of the Montgomery family had taken the news of their father's passing differently, and Junior's already quiet, observant nature had turned somber and silent.

Hailey walked up the few steps to the porch of the two-story home her parents had moved into when she was ten. The inside had changed a few times in almost two decades, but everything on the outside was the same as her earliest memories. The dark-blue siding had faded somewhat, but her mother's perennial flowers looked bright next to the house.

"Hello?" she called inside, pulling her purse off her shoulder and hanging it on a hook in the hall. She threw her keys in the dish on the table next to it and walked around, her heels making a soft click against the hardwood floors.

After checking the living room, kitchen, and family room, she moved upstairs, wondering if anyone was home. It was only one in the afternoon, and while the two youngest Montgomery siblings would usually be in high school, she knew their mother had let them stay home. Even though there was a large age gap between her and the younger two, her parents had always made it a point to treat them all the same and Hailey considered Junior and Penny to be her closest friends.

As she moved down the hallway, she heard a muffled sound. Closing in on the master bedroom, she heard the sound more distinctly. Crying.

She gave the door a light knock and opened it. Her mother was curled up on the large bed.

"Mom? Are you okay?" Hailey strode toward the bed and kicked off her shoes before sitting next to her mother. She pulled her mom's head onto her lap and stroked her shoulder-length light brown hair.

"I'll be fine. I'm just having a moment." She tried to give Hailey a smile, but it looked odd with the puffy redness of her eyes.

A moment for sure. Cari Montgomery was someone who seemed to have it all together all the time. Sometimes Hailey wondered if she'd been adopted, because as hard as she tried to do it all, she fell short more often than not. Her parents, on the other hand, seemed to know the secret of time travel to be able to pack in all that they did. Ballet, basketball, piano, football. Football was always the biggest time-sucker, and a familiar frustration returned at the thought of it.

Seeing her mother cry right then was only one of a handful of times Hailey had seen her cry in her whole life.

"How can I help you?" Hailey reached for a tissue from the night-stand behind her and handed it to her mother.

"Just be here. That's enough." Her mom dabbed under her eyes and wiped her nose, leaving red marks behind.

The guilt Hailey had felt earlier had soured, making her stomach feel like an infected wound. Maybe she needed to be here for her family, even if it wouldn't help herself feel better.

They sat in silence for several moments before her mother spoke again. "I know you're angry."

Hailey groaned. This was not a conversation she wanted to have just now.

"I'm not angry, Mom."

"Yes, you are. You have to know why we didn't tell you. We knew there was nothing we could do. Your dad made it through one more recruiting class, and then he knew that was it."

Heat rose up Hailey's neck, which she tried to tamp back down. Of course, all he thought about was football. But the frustration she might have felt several years ago while hearing that football was his sole focus in life was tempered with the idea that her father wouldn't be there to protect his family anymore. He wouldn't be able to hold her when she cried or call her princess, even if she was too old to hear that. The tears she'd been fighting back all day flowed freely now as she stroked her fingers through her mother's hair.

"That doesn't make it easier, Mom. You could have confided in us long ago, prepared us for what was to come." Her words had a bite to it, and for once, she didn't care. All she wanted was a little more time with her dad so they could talk about anything but football.

"That was your father's decision. He didn't want anyone looking at him with pity, or babying him. It was a challenge these past months to give him as much independence as possible while still hovering."

As much as Hailey tried not to, she snorted. She could visualize that much. Since her apartment was close, she could visit often, but somehow she'd missed seeing any bit of her mother being a helicopter spouse.

Hailey brushed her mom's hair for a moment and then asked, "What will you do now?"

Her mom sat up and looked at her. "What do you mean?"

"I mean, you and Dad did everything together. You traveled with him to so many games. What will you do with your time now?"

Her mom sat up, a large wrinkle creased across her forehead. "I loved your father dearly, and I am so grateful for all the years we had together. But don't think for a minute that I'll sit and have a pity party."

Hailey raised an eyebrow. "What do you call this?"

Her mom swatted her across the shoulder. "It's okay to cry when you've lost the love of your life. And I'll probably have moments like this down the road. But I've got you, Junior, and Penny to worry about." She gave Hailey a half-smile and said, "When you get married, you'll understand what it's like. That you give up parts of yourself to gain so many others. I'm not the same person I was before I met your father, and I'm grateful for that journey."

"You don't ever regret giving up your career?" It was something Hailey wondered about in *her* life. Since her breakup with Avery, her career was most of her identity. She worked so many hours that without real estate, she'd be starting with a blank page.

"No. It's different, staying home and being the support system. But it's what we needed to do. With all the instability of your father's schedule, we needed structure at home." Her mom leaned back on the padded headboard and turned to look at Hailey out of the corner of her eye. "When are you going to get married so I can have some grandkids?"

Hailey rolled her eyes and stood. "Funny, Mom. I seem to be the weirdo magnet, even on the blind dates. If I find a guy who hits all the bullets on my list, it will be a miracle."

"What are you doing to hit the points on a guy's list?" Her mother's eyebrow rose, waiting for an answer.

Hailey scrunched her nose in defeat. She'd never thought of it like that. What was she doing? She worked all the time, so to have fun felt strange. She avoided football like the plague, and her idea of a good weekend was a long bike ride or curling up with a book. Not something most guys were into.

"That's a good question. I'll have to think about it." She turned to walk out the door and said, "I'm going to get something to drink. Do you need anything?"

"No, I'll be down in a minute. We need to go to the airport."

"Why?" Who would be coming into town? Most of the extended family on both sides lived only an hour away at most.

Her mom smiled and said, "Jackson Walker is coming."

Hailey froze. Dad's golden boy? Why?

She'd never met him, but with all the stories her dad told about him, she felt as though she already knew the jerk.

"Is he staying at a hotel near the airport?" Hailey mentally crossed every part of her body, hoping her mother would confirm it.

With a deep frown, her mom said, "He's staying here. And you'd better be nice. That boy has been through a lot."

So had she.

Now she wished she had an excuse to hide out at work. This was going to be a long week.

CHAPTER 3

The flight felt like it had taken forever. Well, flights. That's what happened when a person was traveling around the world, and Jackson knew jet lag was going to hit him hard. It had taken a bit longer than usual to find an available flight out of Australia, and with all the connections and layovers, it had taken over twenty-four hours to arrive at John Wayne Airport. Looking at the date on his phone caused him to do a double take. He'd left Sydney at 4:30 p.m. on Tuesday and had now arrived in California at 5:00 p.m. on Tuesday. Nothing like a eighteen-hour time change to throw him for a loop.

Jackson walked down the stairs to the baggage claim and saw a familiar face smiling at him. "Mrs. M., you didn't have to pick me up. I was thinking I'd get a rental car to get me around town while I'm here."

"Are you kidding? We have two vehicles just sitting around at home. You can use one of ours." She smiled and pulled him in for a hug.

He could see the worry lines around her eyes, and her smile didn't make her face beam like he remembered. Maybe losing a spouse did that to a person—not that he had personal experience witnessing such a thing.

"How long will you be in town?" she asked.

He pulled on the collar of his polo shirt. "Well, that's the thing. I was thinking about staying at the house until the funeral and then getting a hotel. I've got business in town, so I'll be here at least a month."

"Nonsense. You'll stay with us the whole time."

"That's too long, Mrs. M. I don't want to impose." He held up a hand, trying to show her he was serious.

"Like I said before, you're family. Stay as long as you need."

Jackson's emotions had to be checked before he said softly, "I appreciate that." This woman had accepted him into her home on several occasions throughout his tenure at Hawthorne. Every time she mentioned him being a part of her family, the lifelong yearning for family resurfaced. He was still grateful to her for giving him a sense of home he'd never experienced growing up.

The belt of the carousel started to move, and his bags came around. When he pulled them off, he saw her raise an eyebrow.

"Hawaiian flowers?"

With an embarrassed smile, he said, "Yeah. I do quite a bit of traveling, and I've found it's easier to spot these than the generic black ones."

Mrs. M. laughed. "That's a good point. I'll have to remember that for future trips."

She pointed down the hall, and Jackson wheeled the luggage behind him as he followed her. With his laptop bag slung across his shoulder, it didn't feel much different than getting off the plane twelve years ago as a freshman. He'd walked down the same way and had taken one of the shuttles the university sent around. What a difference he felt, walking out of those doors knowing his favorite coach in the world was no longer alive.

Mrs. M. pushed a button on her key fob, and the lights blinked on a small crossover SUV. She opened the trunk, and Jackson lifted his large suitcases inside, having to squeeze them in to get the door closed.

"Did you bring enough shoes?" Mrs. M. asked, a smirk on her face.

Jackson grinned. "No, I left a few at home that I should've packed."

"You pack as much as my daughter Hailey. Then again, you're here for a month. She packs like that for a weekend trip."

Her words caused Jackson's mind to work, trying to recall Hailey. Junior and Penny he remembered, but it had been a couple years since he'd been back, and they'd changed a lot based on their Facebook profiles. But he couldn't remember meeting the oldest daughter, only remembering she looked like an older version of Penny in pictures around the house.

The drive was comfortable as the two of them talked about this and that, catching up. It was when things got more personal that Jackson wished he'd rented his own car. To do that would have hurt her, and during this hard time, that was the last thing he wanted to do.

"So, do you have a girlfriend in Australia?" Mrs. M. turned to him with a smile.

Jackson gulped, not expecting that question so soon. "No, no I don't."

"Whyever not? I'm sure you catch the eye of a lot of girls. Have you—"

"I've been really busy with work the past few years," he said, cutting her off. He didn't need her to ask if he'd tried any dating sites or even went on dates.

Mrs. M. turned into the driveway of the same blue house he remembered, and a dull ache seared his chest. This week was going to hurt, and not physically.

As she put the car in park, she turned to look at him. "Just promise me you'll try to find a girl. As much trouble as they might seem at first, it gets lonely without someone to trust and talk to. With everything you have to deal with for your businesses, someone on your side is the best idea you could have." She reached for his hand, resting hers on top of it. "I'll never regret the time I had with Dan. Even during the last few months through the few treatments he accepted."

"I'm sorry, Mrs. M. I'm sorry I haven't come to visit in so long."

She gave him a close-lipped smile and pulled on the door handle, waving him toward the house. "Let's go in, and we'll come get your things later. I'm sure you're hungry after such a long day of travel."

Actually, days, but who was counting?

He moved behind her, remembering all the talks he'd had with Coach on that front stoop. Life, football, the future. All of it. Jackson pictured what his life would've been like if he'd had someone like Dan Montgomery there from the start. It would have been easier for sure, but would he have understood the sacrifices it took to get to where he was?

They walked in through the living room, which looked exactly the same. The smell of garlic wafted to him, and he felt his stomach rumble. When was the last time he'd eaten a full meal?

Walking into the room, he saw a familiar face, only she stood almost a foot taller than the last time he'd seen her. "Penny?"

"Jackson," she said, her face bright and smiling. "I can't believe you're here. I was beginning to wonder if you were allergic to California or something." She ran up and gave him a hug, leaning up on her tiptoes.

"Not allergic. Just busy." His attention drifted to the pot of noodles on the stove, and his stomach rumbled again, demanding to be fed. "How old are you again?"

"I just turned sixteen! I have to wait for my driver's license, though, because there are a ton of us in the same driver's ed class. Sometimes I wish my birthday had been at the beginning of the school year so I could be the first to drive in my class, but I guess a January birthday is better than May, right?" Her words seemed to tumble out, as if she'd been holding on to them for too long. Jackson's mind was still trying to catch up.

Mrs. M. motioned and said, "Which is why we have extra cars just sitting around. Besides, I get one month without another teenage driver on my insurance."

Glancing at the pot on the stove, Jackson said, "Holy dooley! That smells good enough to eat."

Penny grinned. "I've missed your weird phrases, Jackson. Are you hungry? I made pasta alfredo from scratch." She bounced on her toes, causing Jackson to smile at her enthusiasm.

"She wants to be a chef, so I told her she can show me here to convince me she needs cooking lessons." Mrs. M. twisted her mouth and winked at him in the process.

"So you don't have to do the cooking, huh?" He grinned at Mrs. M., and she did the same back, pointing her finger at him as though that explained everything.

"Where's Junior?" he asked, looking into the family room.

The kitchen went silent, with Penny turning back to stir the sauce and Mrs. M. pulling out some plates. Mrs. M. finally said, "He's been having a rough couple of weeks. Dan and I told the kids about the cancer almost ten days ago, and since then, it's been rare to see him more than just getting off to school in the morning."

Jackson had always had fun with Junior. The younger boy had looked up to him in every aspect. His talents were better suited for basketball than football, but there was a lot he'd try to imitate about Jackson. It had always made Jackson cautious about what he said and did while in the Montgomery home.

Taking a seat at the bar, Jackson watched as the two women moved around the kitchen with ease. It was still a strange sight for him, even after all this time. His mother hadn't been the domestic type, and most of the time, his breakfast, lunch, and dinner had been a box of cereal.

Footsteps sounded from the stairs, and a few seconds later, a girl walked into the kitchen, light brown hair moving behind her. He didn't get a full glance of her face, but he saw her full lips from her profile as she made a beeline for Mrs. M.

"Mom, where is your sewing box? A button just fell off my suit coat."

"Hailey, you need to fix it now? We're about ready to eat." Mrs. M. frowned at her with a hand on hip and eyebrow raised.

Jackson watched as the girl he assumed was Hailey took a slight step back at her mother's body language. He'd done the same on several occasions as a student.

With a quick breath, Hailey said, "I don't want to lose the button before I have a chance to fix it. I'll be five minutes, tops." For a moment, it looked as though there would be a standoff, but then Mrs. M. shrugged, giving Hailey directions to the sewing box in her bedroom closet.

Hailey turned, stopping when her eyes locked on Jackson's.

Mrs. M. moved next to her and said, "Hailey, this is Jackson Walker. Jackson, my oldest daughter, Hailey. You two never met in college, right?"

All Jackson could do was shake his head and keep his mouth closed. With her hair reaching her elbows and her almond-shaped hazel eyes, he had to close his mouth to keep from looking like a drooling creeper.

"I know who he is," she said with a gruff tone. She flashed a fake smile and turned to walk out of the room. Well, at least she looked great on the outside. Her personality, not attractive.

When he heard her steps bounding up the stairs, Mrs. M. said, "Sorry about her. She's got a chip on her shoulder about anything and anyone connected to football or sports in general."

Jackson shook his head, wondering if he'd heard right. "Huh?"

"It's a long story. You'll have to ask her."

That was the last thing he was going to do. Even though he no longer played football, from the looks of her at the mention of him, he wasn't quite sure what she would do if he started the conversation. Keeping his face intact was a new priority now that he'd be staying at the Montgomery house.

CHAPTER 4

*H*ailey moved into her mother's walk-in closet and shut the door. Slammed was more accurate. Jackson did not match the description in her head by a long shot.

Okay, she had to breathe. Relax. He had been a football player.

She felt her body ease up a little, as she'd trained it to do for the last few years when she talked or even thought about football.

The man was gorgeous, she had to admit. His blond hair mixed with his crystal-blue eyes made it seem as if he was staring into her soul. She'd almost felt an electrical shock, but that could've been from standing too close to one of the electrical outlets. He was sitting down, but from the looks of him, he was a lot bigger than most punters. Then again, it had been how many years since her father had coached him?

Focusing on the task at hand, she located her mother's sewing box and sat on the floor. She rifled through it and finally found a lone needle. She pulled out a spool of thread and got to work on the suit coat, finishing within minutes.

She debated whether or not she should go back downstairs. Mr. Ocean Eyes would probably think she was crazy after she'd been so curt. She'd kind of panicked, not realizing her nervous system would go on the fritz just looking at him.

"Dinner's ready," Penny said, opening the door. When she found Hailey on the floor, she raised an eyebrow and asked, "What are you doing in here still?"

Hailey stood up, trying to think of something to say. "I, uh, just finished sewing the button on my coat."

"Please, you've been up here for fifteen minutes. I've seen you sew buttons before, and it's only taken five in the past." A grin spread across Penny's face, and she said, "You're scared of Jackson, aren't you?"

Shaking her head and standing, Hailey said, "No. Of course not."

Penny poked her in the side, causing Hailey to jump. "You are too. You hide whenever you're nervous about something." Wiggling her eyebrows, she said, "He's really hot, isn't he?"

Biting the side of her bottom lip, Hailey nodded.

With a triumphant look on her face, Penny turned, moving toward the bedroom door.

Hailey reached out and grabbed Penny's arm, turning her to face her. "Do not breathe a word of that to anyone, all right? I don't need Mom trying to match us up or anything."

"You could use something to help you loosen up. Maybe hanging out with the fun-loving, charismatic, beautiful guy with an awesome accent would do just that."

Penny spun and ran out the door, leaving Hailey standing still, opening and closing her mouth. Why did she feel like she'd just confessed the wrong thing to the wrong person?

Trudging down the stairs, her stomach growled as she neared the kitchen. The food smelled good, and her sister was definitely improving in her culinary skills. The house wasn't filled with smoke, which was the first good sign. Hailey just hoped it tasted good because she'd forgotten to eat lunch.

Taking one last breath, she stood and walked into the kitchen, determined to escape dinner unscathed and then head back to her apartment as quickly as possible. She was just grateful she had that out. She didn't know how long this guy was staying, but she needed to keep distance between them. As he came into view, she knew she'd either want to strangle him by the end of the trip or kiss those pink lips.

Ugh. Where had that thought come from? He hadn't even said a word to her. She was jumping to the future a little faster than normal, and that wasn't a good sign.

* * *

THE FOOD SMELLED AMAZING, so much better than when Penny had begun cooking three months ago. The smell of garlic and cheese made Hailey's mouth water, and she took a seat across from her mother at the other end of the table. It was where her father usually sat, but she didn't think she'd get through the meal if she had to sit across from the large blond man to her right. This way, he wasn't in direct line of sight.

"This looks delicious, Penny. Alfredo?" she asked, pulling some noodles out of the bowl and setting them on her plate.

"Yep. It was a recipe online I'd been wanting to try. I hope it tastes good." Penny's reservations were understandable as she'd had a couple of meals go horribly wrong. She'd tried to make Chinese food one time and ended up making the house smell like burnt toast for at least two weeks.

"I'm sure it will taste delish," Jackson's deep voice said. He smiled at Penny and winked.

Penny grinned, a small giggle escaping her throat.

It was strange to see their relationship. Hailey had always been gone for the times Jackson had come to their home, usually off to college or avoiding meeting him at all costs. She'd heard enough about him from their father, and when she'd come home, Penny would gush about the handsome football player from Australia. Hailey just thought it was some childhood crush, but she could see how intriguing he could be.

Hailey took the sauce from Penny and ladled it over her noodles.

As she placed the ladle back into the pot, she turned and saw Jackson staring at her. She must have hesitated too long, because he asked, "Do you need help with that?"

She lifted the pot with both hands and reached out to hand it to him, waiting for him to get a good hold on it before she let go, tucking a piece of hair behind her ear. Why did he have to have those piercing blue eyes? It was like a vortex, and she could barely look away.

"How long did it take for you to fly here, Jackson?" Hailey's mom asked.

"Quite a while. The flight to San Francisco was about thirteen hours, and then I had almost a four-hour layover there..." He kept talking but he could have talked about the color of a wall and she'd have been enthralled. That accent was something.

Shaking her head, she twirled some pasta around her fork. The taste was amazing, all the flavors popping out to make the bite rich and delicious.

She should keep thinking about the food. Now she understood why horses needed those blinder things.

"Penny, this is amazing," she told her sister.

Pink rushed to her sister's cheeks, and Hailey grinned at her. As close as they were, sometimes it was hard to connect with the sister thirteen years younger, with all the changes in music and fashion since Hailey was her age, but those little moments meant the world.

Jackson was nodding. "She's right. This is the best pasta I've had in a while. I'm surprised you didn't get it out of a bottle."

"What do you mean?" Hailey asked, breaking her focus to glare at him, feeling herself bristle at the comment.

One of his eyebrows raised, and he said, "You know, prepackaged? Well, I think it's awesome." He stuffed a forkful of pasta in his mouth, and Hailey wondered if it was to avoid the awkwardness.

After a few minutes, her curiosity got the best of her. "What is it that you do in Australia, Jackson?"

"Surf, hike. There's a lot to do where I live."

After swallowing her bite, Hailey said, "No, what do you do for work?"

He grinned as if he'd known what she was getting at the first time. "I own a sporting goods company and then have some other investments."

"Does the sporting goods store take up all of your time?" She couldn't turn off the questions now, feeling like she did when she was getting to know a new client.

"Quite a bit, yeah. I was actually planning to come out here in about two weeks to start looking for some property to open a store here."

Hailey gulped. "You want to open a store here? In Anaheim Hills?"

Jackson left his fork on his plate and sat back, looking at her and shrugging. "I'm not sure yet. I just know I want it somewhere close to here. I have a lot of good memories of college and this part of town, and I thought it might be a good spot to open up shop. Besides, with all the outdoor activities, I'm sure the town and the surrounding areas could support one."

Not just a pretty face. She'd give him that.

"What kind of investments do you have?"

"Hailey, that's enough. Let the poor man eat his food in peace." Her mother turned to Jackson. "I'm sorry. She gets a little curious and likes to ask questions until you're ready to strangle her."

Hailey's mouth dropped open. "I can't believe you said that!"

"What? Jackson is like family. Just because this is your first time meeting him doesn't mean you have to get all irritated about how familiar we are with him. He's been in an airplane and airports for over twenty-four hours. Maybe he just needs to enjoy being in one place for longer than a few minutes."

Dropping her fork on her plate, Hailey stood and said, "Thanks for dinner, Penny." She took her plate over to the sink and washed it before setting it into the dishwasher.

"Where are you going?" Her mother's tone didn't sound friendly, but Hailey turned with a smile.

"I forgot about some work I have to get done at home. I'll check in on you tomorrow." She walked over and kissed her mom on the cheek before moving to give Penny a hug. Then she turned to Jackson, and although she didn't want to say anything, it was as if her mother had tugged on some invisible thread that pulled her manners to the forefront. "It was nice to meet you, Jackson. I'll see you around."

She all but bolted to the door, stuffed her feet into her shoes, and ran to pick up the suit coat from the couch. Her laptop bag hadn't moved from next to the front door. She picked it up on her way out and ran down the porch stairs, the feeling of someone following her urging her on.

She turned the key in the ignition, jumping in her seat as she looked up to see Jackson outside her window. He pointed down, and she pushed the button for the window, curious as to what he would say.

"Hey, I'm sorry about what happened in there just now. I'm an open book for the most part, so if I can answer anything for you, let me know." He smiled at her, melting some of the resolve she'd had to stay away from him.

"Thanks," she finally said. "I ask a lot of questions for my job so I can help my clients get what they want. Sometimes I forget to rein it in." She let out a giggle and then hiccupped, causing him to laugh too. "I've got to get going."

"No problem. I'll see you in the morning, I guess." He took a step back, allowing Hailey to admire the fit of his lime-green t-shirt. He waved and moved back toward the front walk, when Hailey called out to him.

He turned, and she said, "Thanks for being so good to my father. As much as I didn't always appreciate it, you were someone he spoke highly of, and I wanted to thank you for that."

One corner of his mouth turned up, and he nodded. "No problem. He meant more to me than most people will ever know." With that, he jumped up the few steps and disappeared into the house.

As she sat in her driver's seat, she laughed. What was her deal? Was she losing it because she hadn't felt that zing around a man since Avery? Well, this was even stronger than with her ex-boyfriend. She'd have to steer clear of her dad's golden boy. It was the only way to keep her heart guarded.

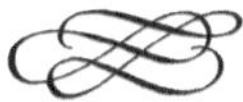

$\mathcal{I}$'m sorry about her," Mrs. M. said as the three of them cleaned up the dishes after dinner.

"It's no problem, Mrs. M. Sounds like she was rather busy anyway." Jackson smiled, reliving the discomfort he'd seen in Hailey's face. He wondered what kind of work she did. Before he had a chance to ask, he heard the front door open and wondered if he would see Hailey again. Something in him jumped at the thought, seeing her face as she thanked him for something he felt indebted to her family for. Her face had softened with the words, and it pulled up several memories of her father giving him advice.

He was more curious about her than he'd been about a girl in some time, and he wondered why, out of all the girls in the world, he was curious about her. Maybe it was because of all the times he'd visited and stayed at the Montgomery home, this was the first time they'd ever met. Her words about not liking the fact that her father talked about him piqued his interest, and he wondered what the story was behind that.

Footsteps came into the kitchen, and Jackson turned to see a tall, lanky young man, his brown hair reaching his shoulders. He flipped his hair to the side, revealing his eyes.

"Junior?" Jackson wasn't quite sure it was the same boy. Obviously, physical appearance and height had changed in just the two years since Jackson had last visited.

"Jackson? I didn't know you were coming." The boy walked forward with his hand out.

Jackson grabbed it, and they pulled each other into a hug, slapping backs.

Stepping back, Junior said, "When did you get in?"

Looking at the clock on the stove, Jackson said, "A bit more than an hour ago. How are you goin'? You're so tall now." Straightening his shoulders, Jackson saw that the younger boy was already an inch taller than him.

"I've been playing basketball with some friends. It's nice to get my mind off of…well, stuff."

Penny moved over to Junior and said, "I made your favorite tonight. I hope you like it."

With a quick smile, Junior nodded at his younger sister. "Thanks. I'm going to take a shower, and then I'll eat." He turned to Jackson and said, "You're not going anywhere, right? We've got a lot of catching up to do. I bet I can smoke you in *Fortnite*."

A deep chuckle escaped Jackson's throat, and he shook his head. "I doubt it, mate. You're looking at the champ of all champs."

"We'll see." The young man smiled before moving out of sight, his feet sounding as he bounded up the stairs overhead.

When Jackson turned to Mrs. M., he was surprised to see her mouth open, and her face looked like she'd seen a ghost. "What is it?"

"He hasn't been that happy-go-lucky since we told him about his father's diagnosis two weeks ago."

Still not sure what it was she was implying, Jackson waited for her to continue.

"Maybe it will be good that you're here. Not that I'm not happy you are, because we all are," she said, as if trying to backpedal. "It's just that we haven't been able to break through to him since then, and I've been worried. Having you here might help him get back into himself."

"Just tell me what to do, and I can do it." He smiled at her, hoping to smooth out the worry lines on her forehead.

Her lips quivered for a moment before she said, "Just be there for him. Listen. He'll tell you soon enough."

She put her hand over her mouth and disappeared, leaving him with Penny in the kitchen. "That meal was way better than anything I could've made, squirt," he said, grinning at her.

Penny laughed. "We need to think of a different nickname. I'm sixteen, and squirt makes me feel like I'm five."

"All right, what about vegemite? That could be endearing."

Turning up her nose, the girl asked, "What is vegemite?"

Smiling, he said, "It's a delicious spread we have out in Australia. I'll have to find some for you to try."

"Sounds disgusting."

"Who knows? You won't know if you like it until you try it." He punched her shoulder softly and grinned.

Rolling her eyes and shaking her head, she said, "Now you just sound like my dad."

That steeled Jackson, a strange emotion hitting him. He'd always wanted to be like Coach Montgomery—well, once he'd finally gotten to know the man. But all Dan Montgomery was and all he had was something Jackson now craved. A home with a wife to come home to, kids running around and telling him about their day.

It was a quick thought, but the rational side of him took over. With all he'd been through growing up, not having the stability he'd always wanted to have, how could he expect to do that to other human beings? He was made for business, for the outdoors, for freedom.

Jackson realized the girl was staring at him like he'd lost his mind, and he made a face, causing her to laugh.

"That's the best compliment anyone's ever given me." He gave her a lopsided grin.

"I'm glad you came to visit, Jackson. It's been a long time." She walked out of the room, leaving him to his thoughts.

Rubbing his hands over his face, he knew he needed sleep. Real sleep to get him over this weird time warp feeling he had. He'd slept well on the plane, but he needed a few more hours of shuteye to get ready for the heartache of the following day.

The funeral was in the morning, and he'd only heard back from a couple of the IBC guys. He hoped most of his frat brothers could make it. Dan Montgomery had made a huge impact on their lives, and thanks to his example and influence, many of them had been successful.

Thinking back to the first time Coach had walked into the frat house still made Jackson cringe. They'd thought they were so tough, that they ruled the world because they were in college and had no one watching them. The day they trashed several hotel rooms was the last "free" day they ever got. And then when Eddie, another frat brother, died in a car accident after driving drunk, taking a family with him, Coach was the one who'd brought them together and mentored them on how to be adults and have fun at the same time.

Jackson wasn't sure how he'd get through the next few days, but he hoped he had a few friends by his side for it.

CHAPTER 6

*H*ailey arrived home and plopped down onto her couch. It was odd to come home before dark, but she'd have to get used to it. For the next two weeks, she'd be stuck doing who knows what. And now that Jackson was staying at her mom's, she couldn't just escape over there whenever she pleased. She'd have to go for a long bike ride or something in the morning. Anything to get her blood pumping and her thoughts cycling through.

Pulling out her laptop, she slid down until her head lay on the armrest. She checked a few emails, but not much had come in. She tried to check her favorite news sites and blogs, but nothing was catching her eye. Something nudged her brain back in the direction of Jackson.

Her heart rate sped up, and she paused, wondering if she really wanted to know more about him. Sure, she felt like she'd heard every story there ever was about her father's favorite player from Australia, and she needed to keep that in mind to make sure she didn't do anything drastic. Like kiss him. But old stories didn't tell her much about who he was now.

She typed his name into the browser and saw a picture of him at the right side of the screen. He was dressed in a tux, his hair slicked back and those crystal-blue eyes looking through her even now. Directing the arrow over to the first link, she clicked, curious as to what it would say.

"Jackson Walker, originally from Tasmania, now lives in Sydney. The owner of CC Sporting Goods, he is also the creator of the headsets used by the NFL, NCAA, and several other organizations internationally. His estimated net worth is in the billions from the investments and inventions we actually know of."

Hailey frowned and sat up, putting her computer on the couch beside her. At least he hadn't lied to them about what he actually did. Her tongue felt like sandpaper, and she moved to the kitchen, hoping a little water would help the bitter taste go away. She'd been around plenty of rich people, had earned sizeable commissions from selling them their dream homes. But she still didn't like to be around them for long periods of time, thanks to Avery and other jerks from Hawthorne.

After a little investigation into her memories, she remembered the reason. It had been her senior year of high school, and her father had made it home early for once, even though it was the middle of the season. But some rich jerk had barged into their home, demanding more playing time for his son, threatening her father's job if he didn't comply.

Her father had always been the special teams coach, so it was a wonder the man didn't go to the coach over the defense, where his son actually played. After a heated debate, the man left, frustrated that her father hadn't given in. It had almost cost her father his job, and although Hailey knew he'd stick to his principles, it would've killed him to leave the school.

And then there was Avery. A talented baseball player from a wealthy family who cared more about appearance and status than a real relationship. He was a professional MLB player for the Angels now, and his net worth was in the millions with his contract and endorsements. But after some of the articles she'd read about his behavior, she'd dodged a bullet and had only realized that after several years and more perspective.

Jackson's face popped back into her mind. He'd just sat there, eating alfredo like it was the greatest thing he'd ever eaten. He'd probably dined in some of the best restaurants throughout the world, and yet he'd been so content in her family's home. Why was that?

Her phone chimed, and she walked over and saw it was her mother. "Hey, Mom. Long time, no talk."

"That's not funny, little lady. I don't know who that was at our house earlier, parading around in a look-alike of you, but you had better not let that happen again. Your father and I didn't raise you to be rude and spoiled."

Heat crept over her cheeks, and she bit her upper lip to keep from making a sound. It had been some time since her mother had corrected her this way, and at twenty-nine, she thought she was past those times. Looking back at her actions just an hour before, guilt blossomed in her chest.

"Mom, I already talked to Jackson. He told me he was fine to answer any questions I had." She wanted to jab the point home that her mother hadn't needed to worry, but she took a breath and contin-ued. "You've all had years to get to know him. If you want me to give him a chance, then just let me have a conversation with him."

Silence followed for a few seconds before her mother said, "I'm sorry, Hailey. I just remembered how frustrated you'd get at any mention of Jackson. I guess I just got worried you'd react the way you always did with your dad."

Leaning her head on the counter next to her half-filled glass of water, she groaned. "Mom, there were a lot of times when I felt like Dad—"

"Would rather be around the frat boys or the football team than with you?"

"How do you do that? I can't even finish a sentence." If her mom could read her that well, did she see some spark of attraction in her at dinner? Hailey hoped she hadn't. That was the last thing she needed.

"I do have ears, you know. Sometimes I wish my brain could be a tape recorder and I could play back things word for word." Her mother breathed in. "You told your dad you didn't want to hear any more about Jackson Walker five years ago. So he kept his promise."

Her mom was good. She had a mind like a steel trap. "Jackson had graduated three years before that. I just couldn't understand why Dad would keep talking about him all the time. It was so frustrating to hear how perfect this guy was when it was tough enough to hear any praise from Dad about anything I did."

"Honey," her mom began, her voice softer now, "you know your father loved you. He was always telling people about your skills to sell a house, a building, or even a cardboard box for that matter."

Hailey couldn't help but laugh at that. She'd only heard him say it once, but she hadn't stopped smiling for a week over it.

"I can still see the disappointment on his face when I told him I was quitting social work. It just seemed like Dad preferred to be at the frat house or on the field instead of with us. And now I find out Jackson is a billionaire…" She growled, not knowing what else to say to that.

"You looked him up, huh? Any interest there?" Even with the slight teasing in her tone, Hailey knew her mother had a slight hope of something. Why had she said anything? Now she'd have to be extra careful about whatever she said about Jackson within earshot of her mother.

Hailey moved to the bathroom and turned on the tub. "No interest there, Mom. He's got a bajillion dollars. What would he need a girl like me for?"

"To have someone who'll be real with him. I can imagine it would be lonely with all that money and no one to share it with. I think you two would be great together."

What? She pulled the phone away from her ear and checked to make sure it was still her mom on the other end. Her mother always had sage advice, but this seemed like something from a sappy love story.

"I've got to go. I'm going to hop in the tub and get some sleep. What do you need help with in the morning?" Hailey could hear a page turning, meaning her mom had pulled out the thick calendar she carried everywhere.

"Nothing. We just all need to get ready for the service. All the details are worked out. With all of the preplanning we'd done, it's made things a lot easier." The last few words broke, and she could hear the emotion in her mom's voice.

Closing her eyes, Hailey debated going back to the house. "It will be all right, Mom. You said so yourself that Dad isn't suffering anymore. I just wish I'd known long enough to shoulder some of the burden."

With a sniffle, her mom said, "Are you ever going to forgive me for that?"

"Yes. I'll just need some time."

Apparently, that was what she needed for every part of her life.

CHAPTER 7

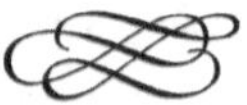

Jackson rose early the next day. He hadn't slept well, especially after Mrs. M. had asked him to speak at the service as they were cleaning up dinner the night before. What could he say about the man who meant everything to him? Who saw past the arrogance and ego of a nineteen-year-old kid and took him under his wing?

All he'd done, all he'd achieved, was due to his surrogate father. He'd never been able to repay all that, and now he never would.

After tying his navy-blue tie, he pulled on his suit coat and buttoned the top buttons. Adjusting a section of hair, he nodded, trying to pump himself for what was to come. He shouldn't be worried. He'd made plenty of speeches, given numerous press releases and interviews. But there was something about coming back to this place, where his roughness hadn't quite been rubbed smooth yet that brought back a wave of nerves.

Stepping out of the room upstairs, he met Junior in the hall, struggling with his tie. Jackson stood before him and took hold of it.

"Wrap the wide part around the narrow until the wide part is in front." Jackson looked up, to find Junior nodding. "Now bring that part behind and up through the hole by your neck. Next, just pull it down through the knot right there and then adjust up."

"Thanks, Jackson. I guess I should probably learn how to do that myself now. My dad always helped me with it."

"No worries. Your father was the one who taught me. He was a good man, Coach." Jackson gave the boy a half-smile, knowing emotions would be on a rollercoaster for most of the day.

Junior nodded and walked down the stairs, slipping on his suit coat. At the bottom, Jackson saw Mrs. M. and Penny dressed in darker-colored dresses. Looking at the older woman, he saw the red nose, the bloodshot eyes, and the bags underneath. It had amazed him that she'd been as strong as she was for so long. Part of him wondered if she was trying to do so for the kids. His gut told him he was right.

The door opened, and Hailey walked in, the curls of her light brown hair falling over her shoulders. She wore a plum-colored dress that fit her curves, hitting her just above the knee.

She turned and, seeing him, took a step back. "Good morning. Are we ready to go?"

Mrs. M. shook her head. "The limo is coming to get us. They should be here any minute." She pulled her wrist up and looked at her watch.

"What if I drive one of the cars? Then you wouldn't be stranded at the funeral home as long." Jackson looked at the members of the Montgomery family one by one.

"You don't want to ride in the limo?" Penny asked, her face showing her shock. To a sixteen-year-old, that was probably a big deal, even though it was for a funeral.

"It's all right. I've gone in a—" His eyes caught onto Hailey's, and she seemed to be studying him even more than she had the other night. "I'll be good." The last words sounded lame to his own ears, but he didn't want to flaunt the fact that he'd been in a limo more times than he could count.

Mrs. M. seemed to agree with his idea and sent Junior back to get a ring of keys. When he returned only a few seconds later, the young man held out the ring and said, "These are for my dad's 4Runner. Just don't screw it up." Junior gave him a wry smile and then hit him in the shoulder.

"Are we sure he should—" Hailey began, pointing to the key ring.

"There's the limo," Penny said, opening the door.

Jackson held it open and motioned for the rest of the family to walk out. Hailey looked at him, the deep line in her forehead causing him to frown as well. He'd thought they'd made progress toward a cordial relationship when he'd gone out to her car the other night. It looked as though it might be more work than he'd expected to get her to trust him. Why she was worth the effort, he hadn't quite figure out but he wanted to at least have the relationship with her that he did with Penny and Junior.

He waited for them get into the limo before he climbed into the older model Toyota. It was clean, to the point that Jackson wondered if the family had it detailed or if this was just the level of cleanliness that Coach had kept recently.

After finding the address on his phone, Jackson made it to the funeral home in less than ten minutes. He pulled the car into the parking spot and got out, looking around to see if he recognized anyone. When he turned and saw his good friend Tristan stepping out of a sleek black rental car, a wide grin split across his face.

Tristan Delacroix was one of his oldest friends. They'd met during rush week their freshman year and had been roommates at the frat house the rest of their time at Hawthorne. They'd been through a lot together, but it had been at least six months or so since they'd seen each other in person instead of through a computer screen.

Tristan saw him and laughed as he walked toward Jackson, pulling him into a crushing hug. Taking a step back, he said with his faint French accent, "My friend, how have you been?"

Jackson held open the funeral home door and motioned for Tristan to walk in, allowing another couple to enter as well. He caught up to Tristan just a few steps down the hall and said, "Just working, mate. I've gotten a lot of surfing in. I've thought about a few techniques and think I know how to help you actually get up on the board and avoid being a shark biscuit." He laughed at the glare his friend cast him.

Tristan raised his hands, shaking his head at the same time. "*Allons-y*. I'm good. This face needs to attract clients we can market for, not scare them away. Which reminds me, we've been going over your numbers again. I've got some ideas to talk to you about on tweaking the campaign for CC Sporting Goods a bit more."

They stopped at the back of the line extending from one of the viewing rooms in the funeral home.

Jackson gave him a half-smile and said, "I remember when you hated advertising. Look at you now."

Tristan chuckled. "Yeah, well, when I don't have my dad breathing down my neck as I work, things are a lot more enjoyable." He tucked his hands into his pockets and said, "Have you made strides on the new headsets for football?"

With a shrug, Jackson said, "We're close but still have quite a few changes to make before they're ready to go out. I'm hoping by next season to have every team outfitted with them."

"Nothing like continually growing the business, right, Jack?" The word sounded more like Jacques.

Jackson chuckled. "Business is good. I have to say it's nice having something in the bank. Better than living off of ramen and cereal."

"Those were character building days, don't you think? I agree, though. Remember how my father wouldn't send more than a couple hundred bucks a month?"

Lifting his chin an inch, Jackson said, "Better than not having anyone send you money." He hadn't meant his tone to be so sharp, but the trace of guilt passed over Tristan's features quickly.

They moved through the line a bit when Tristan changed the topic. "Do you have a girlfriend?" A smug smile was plastered across his face, and Jackson didn't even want to start talking about that non-existent part of his life.

"None of your bizzo. What about you?"

Tristan scrunched his nose and said, "There are a lot of beautiful women in the world, especially in Paris, but I haven't found that one yet." They moved to let some people pass in front of them, joining family members ahead of them. "You're not putting off having a girl-friend just because of—"

Jackson shook his head. "I haven't really had time for girls, to be honest. I take them to benefits and galas, but with all the work I have to do, it's easier to not have someone waiting for me at home."

"It's also lonelier." Leave it to Tristan to be so frank.

"Sounds like not much has changed for either of us."

The line moved up a bit, and Jackson turned as he saw movement out of the corner of his eye. Down the hall, he saw the American twins, Aiden and Evan Pearson, walking toward them.

"Hey, mates! Come join us over here." Jackson waved them over, their smiles visible even down the length of the hall.

"Jackson, Tristan. Man, it's been forever. How are things?" Evan grasped their hands before they pulled together for a back-slapping hug.

Tristan gave them a somber look and said, "It would be nicer to meet under better circumstances. Did you both drive here from Vegas?"

Evan shook his head. "I did. Aiden here moved to San Francisco a few months ago."

Jackson nodded. It was strange that the two of them lived so far apart when they'd been inseparable in college. It was still difficult to tell them apart sometimes, even though he'd spent a lot of time with Evan through football and the frat. Aiden's hair was slightly longer at the moment, which made it easier to know who was who. "How's the Quickstagram founder?"

"Doing well. I've been talking to Tristan about ways to implement it into the marketing strategies for all your companies," Aiden said with a wide smile. He'd always been quieter than Evan, but he still had enough confidence to not be run over.

"Maybe we should hold another conference so we can have a

proper reunion. It's been a while," Tristan said, leaning against the doorframe. The line had hardly moved in the last five minutes.

Jackson turned to Evan and asked, "I take it the resort business is doing well in Vegas?"

Evan grinned. "Yeah, we've seen a significant increase in clients but I swear working is all I do for the most part. It's been a long time since I've actually taken a vacation."

The other three nodded, and Jackson felt the truth of it. He hadn't taken a trip anywhere in the past four years that hadn't been for business in some way.

They'd finally moved into the room, and Jackson looked around the line to see how much longer they'd be waiting.

"Too bad about Mr. M." Aiden's words sounded a little off to Jackson. He'd been so used to calling him Coach that he forgot most of his frat brothers only knew him as Mr. Montgomery. Evan had been a team-mate on the football team, the starting running back. Other than that, the rest of the members of the IBC knew each other from Delta Phi.

Evan wrapped his arm around Jackson's shoulders. "How did you take the news? I know he was like a dad to you."

"It's been a little rough here and there. I guess what hurts the most is that he didn't tell me about the cancer. Mrs. M. phoned me on Monday, well, Sunday in US time. I flew out as soon as I could and contacted all of you."

Evan grinned. "I'm glad you did. After all the man did to get us on the right track, it's the least we can do for him. I don't think I'd be where I am today without everything he taught us."

"Yeah, you'd probably be in jail for something stupid," Tristan said, his shoulders moving as he tried to laugh quietly.

Jackson and Aiden smirked while Evan pretended to be hurt, smiling a few seconds later with a wink. "You know me too well."

They were at the front of the line finally, and Jackson could feel his heart pounding in his chest. He stood back to let the guys speak with Mrs. M. and only glanced into the coffin before stepping to the side. He didn't want to remember Coach this way, gaunt and lifeless. The picture of Dan Montgomery in his head was an upbeat and encouraging man. What would Jackson's life have turned into if Coach hadn't come along?

A tear fell on each side of his face, and he wiped at them with the back of his hand. When he looked up, he saw Hailey, her eyes and nose red. Without even thinking, he wrapped his arms around her and pulled her in. He felt a slight resistance at first, but then she relaxed against him, her body shaking with sobs.

"I'll catch up with you all in a minute," he whispered to his friends as they walked by.

Tristan grinned wide, wiggling an eyebrow, and Jackson looked away, hoping he'd let it go.

Other people milled by, giving their condolences to the family as Hailey cried against him. After a couple of minutes, she pulled back and smiled at him, her sobs quieted.

"Thanks. I'm sorry I got your suit coat all wet." She moved her hand to wipe at the spot.

Jackson looked down, feeling sparks where her hand touched. "It's all right. Sometimes you just need someone to hold on to. I'm sure it's been a long week." His voice dropped to a whisper, and he said, "Your dad meant a lot to all of us. I'm just glad I got to be here." He studied her face, her hazel eyes leaning more toward green. When he broke eye contact, he took in her full red lips, the temptation to kiss her strong.

The funeral director came in and announced it was time to begin the funeral. Jackson turned and gave her a smile before leaving the room. As he walked to the second row in the service room where his friends had taken up most of the seats, he smiled, grateful for the bonds formed in their fraternity. There was nothing but honor in Coach Montgomery's life, and Jackson was ready to celebrate that.

He'd received a text message from Sam earlier that morning saying he couldn't slip away now, as his own mother was having health problems, but the rest of the IBC had made it. Oliver, Roman, Max, Logan, and Gabe sitting down the row past Tristan, Aiden, and Evan. Even though they'd seen each other almost every other year since graduation, it was interesting to see them all dressed up in nice suits compared to their life as college students. From a rambunctious group of college kids to what could now be called some of the most powerful men in their countries.

But it would never have happened without Dan Montgomery. His diligence in helping them right the wrongs, especially after the hotel incident and Eddie's death, was what put them on the right path. He'd taught them how to be gentlemen, how to negotiate, and how to treat others.

The funeral service began, and Jackson felt a slight tremor in his hand. It was the same twitch he had as a student during his public-speaking class. He'd been able to make it through interviews with confidence the past several years. Why would he be reverting now?

Hailey stood to give her speech and Jackson couldn't help but admire her beauty and confidence as she spoke.

"There are so many things to say about my father. He had a passion for football, but more importantly, he cared about people, about serving them and helping them become better. It was something he emphasized in our home all through my childhood and throughout my adult life. There have been many times when I couldn't figure out how to get past a problem, and he always had an answer. Whether it was the one I wanted to hear at the time is a different story." She paused and smiled as wave of laughter passed through the room.

"His passing came as quite a shock to me and my siblings. He decided to forgo all treatments and continue to live until the cancer took over. But he made sure the Hawthorne football team had some great recruits coming in for the new season. We also finally got him to land a month or two ago, which, if you know my father, was a big feat."

Another ripple of laughter broke out, and Jackson noticed the bulk of the noise came from the men to his left.

When she spoke again, her voice had so much emotion that it took time for the words to come out, her gaze staring down at the casket placed before the podium. "I love...you, Daddy. I will miss you until we can see you again."

Jackson studied her, his heart beating a little more rapidly as he did so. He couldn't imagine what she felt. As much as he considered the man they were honoring to be like a father, she was his daughter. To lose someone you love so suddenly had to be rough. The people in Jackson's life had left either before he was born or slowly faded away, leaving him without anything to compare to Hailey's despair.

The director stood behind the podium and said, "Thank you, Hailey. We'll now hear from Jackson Walker. He'll be followed by Mrs. Cari Montgomery before the final song of the services."

Jackson felt his heart in his throat and stood, buttoning his suit coat as he took his place behind the podium.

"This is a bit awkward for me as I've never really been close enough to anyone to speak at a funeral. But I thank Mrs. Montgomery for this opportunity. I'm from Australia, as you can probably tell from the accent." A wave of chuckles went through the room, and he shifted, feeling that comfort ease through him. "I came to Hawthorne University as an eighteen-year-old straight out of foster care. At first, I thought my coming to school in the States was just a bunch of luck falling into place."

Jackson paused, swallowing hard so the mound forming in his throat eased up enough to let him speak. "I got a scholarship which allowed me to get a good education. I was so grateful, and I wanted to do everything right. After a while, I decided that this was the time of my life to have fun and party because I hadn't had that luxury before. But after a few experiences," he paused, turning to look at his frat brothers, "I was taught differently. It was Coach Montgomery who saved my life. I wouldn't be where I am today without his constant guidance, patience, and even disappointments. We'll miss you, Coach."

He moved his jaw back and forth, but he knew that the emotion had seeped in enough that he couldn't speak anymore. Nodding, he looked at the casket before moving back to his seat.

As he sat down, Tristan elbowed him and smiled, tears in his own eyes. Jackson turned his head and caught Hailey looking back at him, a curious expression on her face.

She turned away, and he shook his head. It didn't matter. He didn't need her or anyone else pitying him. He just wished he had one more chance to celebrate with his coach.

CHAPTER 8

Jackson's words felt like a dagger to Hailey's heart. She still didn't know that much about him, but her father had never said anything about him being in foster care. Her original dream since she'd entered middle school had been to be a social worker. But after the emotional rollercoaster she'd felt while in an internship with the local department, she knew she couldn't do it forever. Which is why she'd done something on the opposite end of the spectrum by selling real estate.

She was grateful for the things he'd said and wondered how true it was about her dad saving Jackson's life. Maybe if she'd actually listened to all of the stories her father told about the frat boys he'd mentored, she'd have an inkling of what he meant.

It had been over thirty minutes since he'd held her, but the woodsy scent of his cologne seemed trapped in her nose. She'd been surprised to see the tears in his eyes, but when he'd wrapped his arms around her, she'd felt comfort and protection. Something she thought she'd never feel from a man who wasn't her father, not since Avery had raised his hand against her.

She barely registered her mother's words as her mind was on a high-speeding train of thought. A familiar tune sounded from the piano, and Hailey stood automatically, watching as her brother joined several of the men in well-tailored suits. They picked up the casket and moved out the door, loading it into the back of the hearse.

Hooking arms with Penny, they followed their mother out to the limo and took off toward the cemetery. The service there was short and, thankfully, fairly warm for the middle of winter. Each person stepped forward, laying white tulips on the casket as it was lowered.

After everyone had left and it was just her siblings and her mom, they huddled together. For the first time in a long time, Hailey felt a sense of peace, like this wasn't the end of her life. Nor was it the end of her father's legacy. The weight lifted from her shoulders as she guided her family back to the car.

Exhaustion hit her as she sat in the seat, and all she wanted to do was go home and take a nap.

"I can't believe all but Sam showed up," her mother said, wiping her nose with a tissue. "With them all being so busy, it's a miracle so many of them could get here on such short notice."

"Yeah, it made carrying the casket like lifting a five-pound weight." Junior smiled, and Hailey was grateful to see a hint of light coming back into his eyes.

"Mom," she finally got up the courage to ask, "what did Dad do for them?"

A sad smile stretched over her mother's face. "I don't know the whole story. I just know there was some scandal and each one of those men was struggling with one thing or another when your father took over as the Delta Phi house mentor." The corner of her mouth quivered upward, and she said, "Maybe that's something to ask Jackson when you see him later."

Hailey clenched her teeth, her mind calling up his expression as he'd caught her staring at him after his speech. Those piercing eyes made her skin go all tingly. Staying away from him would be the best idea if she didn't want to get too attached.

Who was she kidding? She pictured the eight guys sitting next to him and knew she was out of their league for sure. Better to keep her distance than to suffer another heartbreak. Once was enough for her.

She kept thinking about the emotion in Jackson's voice as he spoke, and she felt her heart soften toward him. Not enough that she'd go on a date with him, but realizing he had a past that probably wasn't as rosy as she'd assumed of a billionaire had made her more willing to open to him.

The limo pulled into a small reception center in Anaheim Hills, and the four of them got out, the smell of ham and potatoes wafting out to them. As several people approached her mother to give condolences, Hailey leaned in to Penny and said, "I've got to run to the bathroom. Cover for me, will you?" When Penny nodded, Hailey took off in search of solitude.

Instead she bumped into the one person she was trying to avoid.

CHAPTER 9

Not wanting to intrude on the luncheon at the reception hall, Jackson suggested the guys go get some food and catch up. It had been some time since he'd been around, and he turned to Evan for a suggestion.

"There's a place called The Wharf that I've heard a lot about. I haven't had much business up here in a while and haven't visited many of the local haunts."

"As long as it's not all seafood on the menu, I'm fine with it," Tristan said.

Jackson went to pull out his phone and his hand hit the keys in his pocket. "Hey, I forgot I have the keys to the Montgomery's car. Can we swing by and drop them off, mate?" Roman nodded, turning the car around at the next turnoff.

Jumping out of the car, Jackson entered the reception hall and as he turned a corner, he ran into someone. Looking down, he saw a familiar head of brown curls and those almond-shaped hazel eyes looking just as surprised as he was.

"Hailey," he said, his voice softer, almost a whisper.

She turned toward him, an unreadable expression on her face.

"I'm going out with the guys for a bit and wanted to give you the keys in case I don't make it back by the end of your meal." He leaned in a bit, not wanting the woman walking towards them in the hall to hear his next words. "Are you all right?"

A flicker of surprise shone in her eyes, and she blinked, the emotion gone. "Doing better than expected, thank you. Have fun." She gave a small smile and moved toward the bathroom.

Jackson watched her go before turning back and heading out to the car with the guys.

When he slipped back into his seat, Roman asked, "Are you getting cozy with Mr. M.'s daughter?"

The other guys laughed, the loud razzing causing Jackson to shake his head.

An hour later, Jackson and the guys had gone to one of their old haunts for lunch, reminiscing about memories and what they'd been up to since the last time they'd seen each other several months before. They'd just barely ordered when Jackson's phone rang, Mrs. M.'s name popping up on the screen.

"Hey, Mrs. M."

"Where are you? Why didn't any of you come to the luncheon?" He could hear the hurt in her voice, and he felt like he'd been punched in the gut.

Running a hand through his hair, he said, "I'm sorry, Mrs. M. We didn't want to intrude on a family meal, and we figured it would be a good chance for us all to catch up."

"Well, I wish you'd all come. None of you has to fly out tonight, right?"

Jackson pulled his phone away from his mouth and asked the guys, "No one's flights leave tonight, right?"

All of the guys shook their heads.

Bringing the phone back near his mouth, he said, "Looks like we're all in town overnight. What do you need, Mrs, M.?"

"I need you all to come over to the house. Have dinner with us. It would be fun to hear some of your stories with Dan..."

Jackson only heard silence on the other line and had to check that the call hadn't been disconnected. He kept the phone near his mouth and called out, "Mrs. M. wants us all over for dinner tonight. What d'ya say?" He smiled as they all cheered.

Her laugh came through at their response. "Okay, seven o'clock at our house." She sniffed and then said, "Thank you, Jackson. This means a lot to our family to have you all come."

"No problem, Mrs. M. We'll be there. I left the keys with Hailey, but I can be back to drive you home in a bit. Are you done there yet?"

"No, they're just getting started, so take your time. I know you all don't get as much time together as you'd like."

* * *

THE GUYS HAD DROPPED Jackson back off at the reception center at close to three that afternoon. As much as he wished the guys would stop giving him a hard time, he wanted to help make things easier for the Montgomery family and if the only thing he could contribute at the moment was helping with clean-up, then that's what he'd do.

He walked into the building and found the large dining room in the middle, where several people still sat at tables. Some men had already started cleaning up tables and chairs at the other end, and seeing all of the Montgomerys talking to people, he moved over and began carrying chairs to the large racks.

Doing manual labor jobs like this sent him back to the beginning of his career, when he'd done everything he could to scrape by, saving up for all of his research ideas while living on the bare minimum. Sleep had been a luxury that he'd nearly given up during those times, only getting a couple of hours rest before starting the day all over again. He was just glad he didn't have all the trainings he'd had for football during that time.

After another trip to load chairs onto a new rack, he turned, almost running into Hailey. "Sorry about that. I didn't know anyone was behind me." He looked down and saw a chair in her hands. "Let me get that for you." Before she could resist, he turned it upside down and slid it onto the poles, stacking it neatly against the others.

"Thanks. I'm surprised to see you here helping so readily." There was no edge to her words, and it sounded more like a genuine thought than anything malicious.

"I've got to use these muscles for something every once in a while," he said, motioning to his arms. He saw the blush creep up her cheeks and grinned.

"I think we're ready to head out. I assume you need a ride, since you're here?" Hailey raised her eyebrows at him and he laughed, grateful to see her a little off-balance around him.

He gave her a lopsided grin and pulled out a pack of gum. Pulling out a stick, he moved it closer to her and asked, "Would you like a chewie?"

She looked like she'd tried to hide a smile when she said, "Maybe." After she stuck it into her mouth, she asked, "Is that what you really call gum?"

"Yes, it sounds a little better than *gum*, don't you think?" He emphasized the word 'gum' and Hailey hid her mouth behind her hand.

"Let's go, Aussie." With that, she turned and walked in the direction of her mother.

It was several seconds before Jackson realized he'd been watching her with an undivided interest. Shaking his head, he mentally chastised himself. He was here for her father's funeral and then to look for property for his new store. It wasn't worth risking his feelings when an across-the-world relationship was sure to fail.

CHAPTER 10

*H*ailey was excited when they finally arrived at her parents' house. Her mother had debated whether or not pizza would be good enough for the number of people coming to the house, and she'd never been so grateful to anyone as she was to Jackson for saying pizza would be the best idea, especially if it was from Sauce-alito. It was a place that was popular with the college students, and even Hailey felt a bit nostalgic seeing the green writing on the white pizza boxes.

Jackson pulled up the drive, and Hailey saw that the guys had already arrived, sitting or standing around the front porch.

"Looks like they're all early," she said, noting it was a quarter to seven.

"Which means they're on time," Jackson said with a grin. He cocked his head to the side and gave her a look that said she should know what he was talking about. "Your father always said that arriving on time wasn't good enough. 'Impressions are made by arriving early and prepared.'"

Hailey couldn't pull her eyes away from his lips, feeling a chill run through her at his remembrance of her father's words. It was something she hadn't thought of in some weeks, but looking at all of the men, it seemed they'd learned a few things from her father.

Penny and Junior were already out of the car, and Hailey joined her mother and Jackson as they moved toward the trunk.

Looking at Hailey, Jackson said, "Why don't you go get some drinks and plates out? The guys and I will get this." The look on his face wasn't boastful, and Hailey nodded, pulling her mom and sister along with her.

Three of the guys were already waiting behind them and were soon taking the several boxes from the trunk and walking into the house. It took a few minutes to get everything spread out across the island, but the guys were all patient and tried to help out as best they could in the smaller space.

Hailey stood to the side as her mother told the guys to eat up, but none of them moved.

The French guy stepped forward and said, "Go ahead, Mrs. M. Your family should go first."

Her mother tried to argue a bit but finally conceded, and Hailey followed, with Penny right behind her. Taking her plate and sitting at one of the foldup tables they'd pulled from the garage, she watched as the guys finally descended on the food. Something about the whole situation had her stumped, and confusion flowed through her. Maybe she just hadn't met guys outside of her family that didn't consider themselves first in all things.

Jackson slid into the seat next to her, taking a bite from his combination pizza.

Leaning over, Hailey whispered, "What is with the waiting until we all went through to eat?"

Giving her that half-grin that sent her stomach flipping, he leaned closer, and his cologne filtered over to her once again. "Women go first."

When she gave him a look, he smiled wider and said, "One of Coach's rules."

Had her father really had such an impact on that many people? A few more guys filled up their table, and the others sat around the regular dining table.

She was grateful when Jackson made introductions.

"Next to me is Max. He's from Germany. At the end of the table are Evan and Aiden, identical twins, so we can never really tell them apart—"

"Really, Jackson? You should know I'm the one with the best looks," one of them said.

Jackson chuckled, and Hailey couldn't help but smile. "Evan played football with me, so we got plenty of face time with Coach between practices and frat time." He pointed to one of the guys on the other side. "That's Oliver from the Czech Republic. And this here is Tristan from France. Logan, Gabe and Roman are all over at the other table. Sam was the only one who couldn't make it up from Argentina. Everyone, this is Hailey."

The guy named Max had narrowed his eyes at her while chewing a piece of his pizza. "I think I had a class or two with you. Psychology and probably a business class. I'm surprised I didn't put it together that you were Mr. M.'s daughter."

Hailey rolled her lips in, trying to see if his face sparked any memories. "It's possible. That was a while ago, though."

"You went to Hawthorne?" Oliver asked.

Nodding, Hailey said, "It's hard to pass up free tuition."

"Coach might have mentioned it, but I don't remember seeing you there." Jackson chewed slowly, as if trying to remember.

"You also just met me yesterday, so you probably wouldn't have known to connect me with my father. I avoided the athlete area as well as anything close to Delta Phi. I heard enough about you all at home. I didn't need to worry about running into you on campus."

The conversation turned to other things, and Tristan said, "It's nice to go out and not feel like it's a business meeting. It's been a while."

"Agreed," Oliver said. "I'm enjoying the fact that we're not talking or looking at each other through a screen."

Jackson turned to him with a frown. "Your business is phones, Ollie."

"Telecommunications. Yeah, but sometimes even I need a break from it." Oliver gave him a look and took a drink from his glass.

The twin who'd spoken up earlier grinned. "It has been a while since we've gotten together. Are we planning something for later this year? I could use another excuse to get away from work."

"What are you talking about? We spent two days together three months ago when we were in Paris for Tristan's marketing conference." Max's eyebrows had joined, making it look like a skinny caterpillar against the pale forehead.

Hailey had to take a drink to avoid from laughing out loud. Leaning forward, she looked around at the guys as she asked, "What is the IBC? Because the only thing I can think of is the root beer brand."

Max and a few others around the table made noises of disgust. "Root beer is disgusting," he said. "Which is something I said when we formed the IBC three years ago. It stands for International Billionaire Club."

Hailey's jaw dropped open. Pointing to the guys around the table, she said, "You're all billionaires?"

The guys all nodded.

Tristan spoke up. "Probably not a typical occurrence, but we've somehow managed to reach that status in different areas. Max owns several supermarket chains. I'm in marketing. Evan down there runs a few resorts. Ollie runs a telecom company in Europe."

"But how?" Hailey wished her brain would clear up a bit to help her say something more eloquent.

Jackson leaned forward and grinned. "We attribute a lot of it to your father. We could've thrown our lives away in college, but he took care of us, taught us the tough lessons and made sure we knew how to treat people."

Hailey sat in her chair, stunned. What were the odds that ten guys who'd gone to college together would all be billionaires? And each one of them had better manners than all of the men she'd met or dated combined. Turning to look at Jackson, she felt a strange pull in his direction. He had several more qualities she admired besides being attractive. His thoughtfulness and laughter made it so she wanted to be near him, and with an accent like that, she could listen all day. But he would be heading home soon enough, and her life was here. She'd have to tread carefully for the rest of his trip.

CHAPTER 11

After Hailey had gone home and Mrs. M. went to bed, the guys hung out in the family room for a bit longer, some of them playing video games against Junior. Penny had fallen asleep against Jackson's shoulder some time before, and he tried not to move so he wouldn't wake her.

"What's going on with you and Coach's daughter?" Evan asked, giving Jackson a sly smile.

Everyone paused, their heads turned in Jackson's direction. Even Junior turned, a slight smile on his lips.

He tugged at his collar and then looked at the TV. "Nothing is going on with me and Hailey. I just met her yesterday, and she's not digging me. That's for sure."

"Maybe it's because you're a football player," Aiden said.

"Ex-football player," Jackson clarified.

Tristan shook his head. "Just because Katie O'Brien said that while she was making a move on one of your teammates doesn't make it true. Once a player, always a player. I bet she's kicking herself now."

"Yeah, Justin Phillipe played one year in the NFL. You took what life gave you and made gold." Evan gave him a reassuring grin.

"Thanks, guys. She's in the past. I'm just taking life one day at a time." Jackson guided Penny's head to his lap so she could stretch out on the couch and he could move his arms. It had been several years he'd thought of his ex-girlfriend, and the thought of her now made his stomach churn.

"So, what have you got to lose?" Evan asked. "Go after Hailey. From everything I've heard and read about her, she's pretty amazing in the real estate world. And with Mr. M. as a father, she's probably got a good head on her shoulders."

Her face popped into Jackson's mind. Something about her intrigued him. It could be that she'd done nothing but push him away since the moment he'd arrived. But part of him was curious about her. As he thought over how much time he'd be in California, his mind brought back Evan's words about her being a real estate agent.

Leaning forward, Jackson asked, "She's a real estate agent?"

Evan smiled and said, "Yeah. Are you really going to go for it?"

With a shrug, Jackson said, "I'm staying for a few more weeks to find property to set up a CC Sporting Goods here in Anaheim Hills. I can get to know her a little better and see if there is something there." He paused a moment and Junior grinned at him, like that was the best idea he'd ever had. Looking at all of his frat brothers, he asked, "None of you have girlfriends?" All of the others shook their heads.

Tristan spoke first. "Work takes up so much time. It's been a while since I've had a date."

"Are you still pining for Camila? That was years ago, and I thought we helped you through all that." Aiden's voice sounded irritated, and everyone stopped to look at him, the twin who was usually not that blunt.

"Nah, she's one of those 'I think I dodged a bullet' kind of people. Have you found anyone who doesn't want to be with you for your money?" Tristan's voice had an edge to it, as though warning not to mess with him. Each of the guys seemed to ponder that before nodding.

Ollie put his hands behind his head and leaned back. "That is a real issue. If only we could find someone who didn't know who we are, it would be a lot easier."

The rest of the guys agreed, and Junior looked like he was confused as he tried to listen and navigate through his racing game against Evan.

Jackson couldn't help but think about that. The chances of finding a girl who didn't know a lot about him were slim, but as he thought about Hailey, the kind of girl who just wanted to take care of her family, a sliver of hope filled his chest that there just might be a girl out there who wouldn't care about what was in the bank.

Looking at Evan, he asked, "You said Hailey is a real estate agent. Do you know which brokerage she works for?"

ailey's phone went off the next morning, waking her up from a dead sleep. She reached for it on the nightstand, pulling it an inch or two away from her eyes to be able to read her boss's name.

Why would he be calling her this early? She'd only been out of the office three days. Did they miss her that much? Something in her dared to hope he'd called to let her out of her banishment. She could use something to combat the alternation between mourning the loss of her dad and boredom at having nothing to do.

Answering before the call went to voicemail, she said, "Hello?"

"Hey, Hailey. How was your father's funeral? I was going to try to make it, but I had to put fires out all day and missed it." Jonathan sounded a little too happy this early in the morning.

"It was good. A lot of people showed up." She scrubbed her hands over her face, trying to wake up.

"I don't have a whole lot of time this morning, but I just wanted to see if you'd be up for taking on a special client?"

Special client? Since when did they have those? "What is the assignment?"

"I have a man looking for retail space, and he requested the best agent we had. He says he's willing to spend a little to find the right property, and you're our best bet. Are you willing to take it on?"

Her immediate answer was yes, but she didn't want to seem too eager. Ten more days without a work schedule might send her to a crazy farm. "Yeah, I think I can do that. When does he want to start looking?"

"Later today, if possible. I know how much you were looking forward to your mandatory vacation, but this sounds too good to pass up. He's only in town for a short while and wants to make sure he's seen enough properties to make a good decision. If you play your cards right, you might even be selling a house as well." Jonathan chuckled, and Hailey groaned.

Her boss was a likeable guy, but the one thing that irked her was when he thought of clients only in terms of dollar amounts. A sizeable commission wasn't the worst thing that could happen to Hailey, but it was more of a thrill to know she'd found something her clients could love for years to come.

"I can meet at the office just after lunch. Is that soon enough?"

"Perfect. I'll let him know."

Hailey looked at the clock on her wall, calculating the things she needed to do before she went to the office. "Is he looking for property just around Anaheim, or do you have a radius I can do some preliminary checks on?"

"I'll have to ask him, but I think if it's twenty-five miles or so from Anaheim Hills, you'd be safe. Start there, and you can refine your search once you meet." The man paused for a second before saying, "You'll let me know if you can't handle this, right? I just want to make sure you are getting the rest you need."

Hailey scoffed. "I'll be fine. Besides, you still have all of my other client files, and I'm assuming you won't let me work on those at the same time."

"No, I will not. This account could mean big things for our company. Treat him right and make him happy."

"That's what I always do," she said in a sing-song voice.

Hanging up the phone, she glanced at the mirror hung across from her bed and realized she needed to hop in the shower to get ready for this meeting. Then she'd run a search of nearby commercial properties before she met the man. Being prepared always made her look better than when she walked in with no ideas whatsoever.

* * *

HAILEY WALKED into the real estate office a few hours later, bringing a small tray of drinks for the few people she usually saw in the mornings. The receptionist thanked her over and over again, and her boss was pleased. She had to keep him happy until she could get back to work full time, and this was a surefire way to do it.

"Am I late or is he?" she asked, as she walked into Jonathan's office.

"It looks like he's just walking in." Her boss pointed behind her, straight through the wall of windows that encompassed the large corner office.

Hailey turned, her eyes taking a second to see through the glare of the window. As she focused on the Australian with the knee-weakening blue eyes, her heart sped up as though she'd started sprinting. Part of her was almost excited that the special client was Jackson, while the other part of her wondered if she'd be better off finishing out her mandatory vacation.

Jonathan led her out of the office, and they met Jackson halfway down the hall.

"Jackson Walker, meet Hailey Montgomery."

Hailey bit the side of her cheek before saying, "Yeah, we already know each other." When her boss looked at her with a curious expression, she said, "He played for my father at Hawthorne."

"That's incredible! What a small world. Well, I've got a conference call in a few minutes, so I'll leave you to figure out how to help Mr. Walker. Good luck." Jonathan smiled and moved back into his office, leaving an awkward tension in his wake.

Tucking a piece of hair behind her ear, she glanced up, wishing she'd missed the phone call that morning. "I didn't realize it would be you."

"I asked him for the best real estate agent in his office, and I'm guessing that's you. Where do we start?" Jackson winked at her, causing her to turn on her heel and walk back down the hall. She didn't go as far as her boss's office but turned left before it. When she looked back, she saw him still rooted to the spot, a puzzled expression on his face.

"Let's get started. I've got some things in my office." She waved him over and couldn't pull her eyes away as he moved down the hall. He was dressed in a navy-blue polo shirt with well-cut jeans and what looked to be boots on his feet. Her eyes trailed back up to his face, where the hint of a smile played at his lips.

Taking a deep breath, Hailey moved behind her desk, motioning toward the chair on the other side. "Take a seat. We can go over some of the needs, wants, or whatever it is you envision for this space. Then I can look up some places, and we'll check them out later this week."

Jackson nodded, sitting down in the chair. "I'm surprised you're back to work so soon after the funeral." His head was cocked to the side, and from the questioning tone of his voice, she had to bite her tongue to keep some choice words from coming out. Who was he to say whether or not she should be back at work or not? As good as he looked, he still pushed her buttons.

"Actually, I was supposed to have another ten days off, but because Jonathan has deemed you a 'special client,' he's allowed me to come in to work with you." She focused on a spot on the wall behind him, making it look as though she was studying his hair.

"I'm the only client you're working with right now?" His jaw moved side to side, and she wondered what kind of scheme he was concocting.

"Maybe." She brushed her hair back over her shoulder and pulled out her preliminary information sheet. She'd use it throughout the process, helping to keep details fresh in her mind. Pulling out a pen, she said, "Okay, this property is for your sporting goods store, correct?"

Jackson smiled and nodded, a business façade taking over his features. "Yes. It needs to be at least four thousand square feet. As far as radius, I'd like to stay within twenty-five to thirty miles of Anaheim Hills."

"Most of the bigger businesses are better sustained in a larger city. Anaheim Hills wouldn't be able to sustain a store as big as yours." She looked at him, trying to make it seem like she was no-nonsense, all the while her insides were on the fritz.

He leaned forward, staring at her with those ice-blue eyes, causing her stomach to flip. "Believe it or not, I have done some research on my own. You don't think I'd set up a store across the world on a whim, do you?"

Even though his tone was soft, lighthearted, Hailey felt her defenses rise, irritation that she'd even been thinking he was attractive.

He continued as she fumed. "The store I have in mind for this area is smaller than the ones in Australia, but they would carry just about everything those do, just fewer of each product. At least until we gain traction here."

Hailey wrote down a few notes, hoping to keep her mouth shut as much as possible. She worked to keep her face neutral, knowing that the first meeting was the best time to get all the information, hopefully shortening the amount of time they'd have to spend together. Somehow he knew how to make her feel as if she were six inches tall.

She looked up, raising her eyebrows and said, "Anything else?"

"Other than that, I'm pretty flexible."

The word sent off warning bells in her head. She'd heard that often from previous clients, and that usually signaled the clients who couldn't make a decision or who tried to sound reasonable but were nitpicky about everything they saw.

She forced a grin and said, "Okay. I pulled up some commercial spaces this morning, but several of those are not large enough and outside the range you gave me. Let's see, tomorrow is Friday. Do you mind if we meet in the morning so I can research the places and we can start looking?"

"That would be great, and thank you for helping me. Do you want to meet here?"

Hailey thought about that for a moment. "Maybe let's meet at my mom's house. Eight in the morning?"

"Works for me, Hailey. I'll see you then." He nodded to her before standing and walking out.

Her office wasn't surrounded by glass, but it had a large piece of it in the wall facing the reception desk. She watched him walk all the way to the elevator and until the doors closed.

Sinking back into her seat, she groaned. This was going to be bad. She had to be nice to him, and she had to make sure she found him a good retail spot; otherwise, her boss and her mom would never forgive her. She had to find a way out.

Walking over to Jonathan's office, she straightened her shoulders and barged in. "I can't help him."

Her boss looked up from some paperwork and frowned. "What do you mean, 'I can't help him?' Of anyone in this office, Jackson Walker should be a homerun for you."

Eyebrows furrowed, Hailey rested her hand on her hip and said, "I can't cite conflict of interest or something?"

"You're breaking no rules here. Just because your father coached him in football doesn't mean you can't do your job."

"I just...there's just—"

"The board is thinking of bringing on another broker. If you want that spot, you'll see this through to the end."

He'd hit on a soft spot, and from the satisfied look on his face, he knew it. As much as she wanted to say no, broker was her dream position. Sure, she had enough years of experience to go out and start her own brokerage, but that would take months, years even, to get the ball completely rolling. Being a broker in a well-established business would make her life that much easier.

"Fine. I'll do it. Just know I'm not happy about it." Yeah, that didn't sound like she was a five-year-old.

Her boss nodded, his smug smile causing her frown to deepen.

She turned and walked back to her office, trying to focus on the task at hand.

After a few minutes, she grabbed her purse. She knew she

wouldn't be able to work here for the rest of the day. Taking the few paper sheets she'd printed out earlier, she walked out, determined to get some food and then curl up with her laptop in her apartment.

Walking out of the building, she tried to focus on her job, but little memories of Jackson flashed through her mind. After all the little things he'd done, like cleaning up after dinner or connecting with Junior, it was getting harder to avoid his little charms. As she thought over the conversation they'd had minutes before, he hadn't been rude or a jerk. He was a businessman, and she should have thought of that before she got all offended.

Blowing out a breath, she wished she could rewind and redo the morning from start. She got in her car and placed her purse and the papers on the passenger seat, willing her brain to remember some property that might work for his store. She needed to find the perfect location as soon as possible in the hopes of being rid of that blond Australian heartbreaker as quickly as possible.

CHAPTER 13

Jackson smiled as he pulled on a t-shirt and some board shorts. He knew Hailey was coming over, and for some reason that filled his stomach with honeybees stinging in spots here and there. What was it about that girl that was so different than all the others? Maybe the fact that she didn't fawn all over him? Not that he particularly enjoyed that kind of attention, but it was refreshing to have someone treat him as a real person instead of some celebrity.

He fixed his hair and brushed his teeth and was walking down the stairs just as Hailey walked through the door. "Good morning," he said.

She nodded and moved toward the kitchen, not even waving him to follow. He did anyway and saw her setting up shop on the kitchen table, placing a stack of papers next to a notebook and her laptop. She sat out a pen and a pencil, moving them several times until they were straight, and then sat down.

"What are you doing?" He looked at her with his eyebrows raised and scratched near his jaw line.

"Setting up to go through all of the properties I found." She patted the table next to her as if to tell him to sit down.

He shook his head. "I prefer to see them in person, if you don't mind. There is only so much you can learn about from photos. I've been through several buildings where the owner had paid the photographer to doctor them up, making them look much nicer than they were in person."

The more time he had to spend with her, the better chance he had of winning her over, at least to being friends. Playing the demanding client could possibly backfire on him, but he figured this was his best opportunity.

A frown covered her face, and he had to hide his smile. She was so cute when she was mad.

When she spoke, it was through clenched teeth. "What I usually like to do with clients is find a handful of properties that fit all of their wants and then we go visit them. So, I've pulled about fifteen that meet your criteria, and I thought we would narrow it down to four or five." She pressed her lips together in a tight line.

He couldn't help but let the sides of his lips turn up. Maybe he could charm her. "Okay, are there any that are under four thousand square feet?"

She looked through the papers and nodded.

"Cut them out. It will already be a stretch for such limited space, so let's not worry about anything smaller."

Her shoulders relaxed a bit. She pulled out three listings and set them in a pile to the side. Looking up at him, she raised an eyebrow. "Anything else you can think of?"

Deciding to take a seat, he took the larger pile of papers and looked through them quickly. He pulled out four properties and set them down with the other three she'd already pulled out. Two were several miles outside of the area he wanted. The other two were multiple floors, and he preferred to keep it to one.

"Let's go see these," he said, handing the leftover pile back to her.

She narrowed her eyes, glancing between him and the papers. "You're saying we should go see *all* of these properties?" She looked as if she was ready to take his head off. So much for charm. Finding a way to get her to open up was going to be a lot harder than he imagined.

"Yeah, that way I can get ideas as we go along. Some of my greatest successes have come from just moving along and being in the right place at the right time." Grinning at her, he said, "At least we cut the number in half."

Her jaw wiggled, and she looked down at the listings. After a few moments, she started arranging them.

Jackson was curious and moved next to her, looking over her shoulder.

"I've got them all arranged by location so we won't be driving all over Southern California. Should we get started?" She gave him a close-lipped smile, and he nodded.

After packing up her laptop, they moved down the hall. Jackson moved in front of her, opening the front door and waving her through. She stared at him for several seconds before continuing through, the confusion on her face making it hard for Jackson to know what she was thinking.

As they walked out to the car, he touched her shoulder lightly. She turned toward him, looking annoyed.

"I'm sorry, Hailey. I don't mean to be a pain. I just like to be informed about big decisions like this. I can go look at the properties without you if you need to do something else."

She rubbed her lips together, probably to give herself time to think. "No, I don't have anything I need to do. You're right. The more you see, the better you'll know which one will work or not."

They made it to the car, and he opened the driver's side of her car. Her eyebrow raised, and she asked, "Why did you do that?" She looked between him and the door, which helped Jackson get her meaning.

Shrugging, Jackson said, "It's just something I do. It was one of the things your father taught me."

She stared at him for several seconds before sliding into her seat, allowing Jackson to close the door. When he made it around to his side, he sat down and looked over at her, only to find tears sliding down her cheeks.

"Are you all right? Did I say something wrong?" Jackson turned toward her, unsure what to do. It had been a long time since he'd seen a woman cry, besides Mrs. M., and he felt panicky, not knowing how to help.

Hailey wiped at the tears and sniffed. After taking a deep breath, she turned to look at him, with a sad smile. "No, you didn't do anything wrong. It's just the little things that hit me every once in a while. My dad would always open doors for my mom. I confronted him about it once, telling him we didn't live in the 50s." Her smile widened, and she shook her head.

"I can imagine that didn't go over very well." Jackson grinned back, thinking of a time when he'd done the same.

Hailey shook her head. "He said that it didn't matter what decade it was, that a man should always treat a woman with the respect she deserved. Then he said that love was in the little things. I didn't realize what he meant until now."

Jackson wanted to ask her what she meant by that, curious if it had something to do with him. Deciding to let it be, he turned to look forward while he buckled his seatbelt. Maybe she'd open up a bit more throughout their travels that day.

* * *

HAILEY FELT LIGHTER than she had in some time as she pulled out of her mother's driveway. The way Jackson had given her a look of panic when he'd seen her crying pricked her heart, and she had to do her best to keep her eyes on the road. His cologne seemed even stronger in the small space of her car, and she felt a tingle zip through her.

She was just glad her mother couldn't see her right then. That was all she needed. Her mom jumping to conclusions and thinking that she was going to fall in love with Jackson. Sure, his accent was adorable, and the dimple in his cheek was eye-catching. That didn't even encompass the crystal-blue eyes. From all she'd learned about him over the past few days, she hadn't scratched the surface of who this guy really was, and part of her was ready to dig deeper, even if her heart was in danger of forming an attachment.

"Our first property is just over here on Main Street. It was once a used bookstore but has sat empty for the last year." She pulled alongside the curb and pointed to the building on Jackson's side. "It's about forty-three hundred square feet. Should we check it out?"

"I'm ready." He smiled and got out of the car, Hailey following close behind. She watched as he looked up at the building and then turned to look at her. "What happened to the bookstore?"

Hailey racked her brain for the answer. She knew it wasn't in the listing notes, but she'd lived there long enough to have heard something about it.

"I can't remember exactly, but I think the owner passed away and his kids decided not to continue the business." She unlocked the realtor box, pulling out the key. After she opened the door, they walked in, each glancing at one part or another.

Jackson walked to one wall, grasping one of the shelves and shaking it a bit. "The built-in shelving is a bonus. I'd just need to order something similar to match for the shelving in the middle, which wouldn't be a problem."

Standing in the middle of the room, Hailey smiled as a few distant memories surfaced. "My mother used to bring me here. She'd let me sit in the children's section while she went to find her 'kissing books,' as she'd called them. There was a stuffed chair there in the corner, and I'd pile up as many books as I could carry on a small table right in front of it."

She felt sadness at the loss of such a place in the community, but if Jackson could put the building to use again, maybe it would start a new chapter of memories.

When she glanced over at him, she saw that his features had softened, his jaw not showing the tension it usually did.

"It's times like these when I wish I had memories of something like that. I wasn't taken places very often as a kid." His lips twisted to the side, and he turned, trying to hide the emotions playing on his face.

Hailey held back, allowing him to look around the room and in the back. When he reappeared, he looked like he'd composed himself, flashing her a grin as he walked toward her. What had he gone through? From the little snippets she'd picked up, his childhood hadn't been easy, which made her feel bad for judging him over and over again.

"It has potential, but I'd like to see the others to compare." He moved past her toward the door, holding it open for her.

"We can do that. The next one is just a few blocks over."

CHAPTER 14

Jackson liked the first property, but part of him wondered if he felt that way because of Hailey's memories of the place. He hadn't meant to share anything about his childhood, but the way her face had lit up with the memory, it was difficult to keep his own from surfacing.

He didn't remember much about his biological mother, but running errands with his foster mothers wasn't something he'd ever done. He'd spent a lot of time in the libraries near each foster home, but nothing as sentimental as what she'd shared.

They spent the next couple of hours visiting four other properties she'd pulled from the real estate system, and in all honesty, none of them felt like the one they'd seen first.

"Should we stop and get something to eat?" he asked her after the last one had been full of spider webs.

"That would be great," she said right as her stomach growled. The two of them chuckled over that for a moment as they got into the car.

Jackson turned and asked, "Is there somewhere you recommend? It's been quite some time since I've lived here, and I'm sure there have been a lot of changes."

"What kind of food do you like?"

"Pretty much anything. It took me a while to get used to the flavors of Indian food, but it's one of my favorites now."

She grimaced, and he couldn't help but laugh. "That stuff is not good."

"What do you like, then?" They got into the car and sat for a few seconds to think on it.

Hailey started up the ignition and tapped her finger on her mouth. "I'm not really sure. I've never really branched out to the more exotic kinds of foods."

"So, have you tried Indian food?"

She scrunched her nose up and said, "No?" The question at the end of it made her sound as though she were being punished.

"We should try it, if you want to. They've got to have something here in town." He looked at her, seeing her discomfort. "Is there a place you'd like to go?"

Hailey bit her bottom lip. "I can't think of any. Are you sure I won't die if we try it?"

Jackson grinned and reached out to touch her arm. "I promise you'll be fine. Is it the spicy you don't like?"

"It just looks like a lot of flavors I'm not used to. My mom has always been a meat-and-potatoes kind of cook. Now, with Penny cooking, we've branched out to a few new things, but I still haven't tried a lot.

"Then you're with the perfect guy...I mean, what I meant to say was I have tried a lot of foods and can help you find something you like." He took out his phone, hoping to hide his embarrassment over such a slip, and searched for a restaurant. "Looks like we're only a few klicks down from a place. Just take a left up there at the roundabout."

"Roundabout? Klicks?" She laughed, causing Jackson to look ahead, squinting to see what was ahead of them.

"That is definitely not a roundabout. Just turn left at the stop sign." After a few seconds, he turned to look at her. "You do know what a roundabout is, right?"

Hailey gave him a sheepish grin and shook her head. "I've heard about them, but we don't have any around here."

"That's one of our favorite things in Australia. I like it because I don't have to stop." He directed her again and then said, "Klick is for the distance, usually in kilometers."

With a smile, she said, "Interesting. It's crazy how we speak the same language but a lot of the words and meaning are different."

Once they got to the restaurant, Hailey's eyes looked like saucers, and the menu overwhelmed her. He could see it in her body language as she shifted several times while trying to decide.

Leaning forward on the table, Jackson put his hands closer to hers. "The big question is, do you like spicy foods?"

"No. My tongue always feels like it'll fall off."

"Can you handle even a little bit?" He turned his head to the side, trying to get a good read on her emotions.

She tucked her hair behind her ear, something he'd noticed she did when she was nervous or trying to give herself some time to think. "I guess I can try."

"You don't have to. I just wanted to gauge what would be best for you."

Raising her hands at her sides, she said, "I trust you."

The sound of those words coming from her lips caused him to stare at her for a few seconds longer, surprised to hear something like that from her. She'd seemed so set against him when he first arrived, and with the tumult of emotions he was feeling toward her, he was grateful to see her feelings regarding him had changed, if only slightly.

The waiter walked up, and Jackson said, "I'll take the tikka masala, and the lady will have butter chicken. We'd like a side of naan bread as well, plain and garlic. I'll have a Sprite." He paused and looked toward her. "Do you want anything to drink?"

"Root beer?"

Jackson couldn't help but laugh, remembering Max's comment at dinner after the funeral.

Hailey folded her arms across her chest and asked in a defensive tone, "What's so funny?"

Raising a hand, Jackson nodded to the waiter, and the man moved away. Turning to Hailey, he said, "I'm so sorry. It just made me think of Max's comment the other night when we were eating at your parents' house. He is not a fan."

"Yeah, I didn't quite get that. Do you not have root beer in Australia?" She leaned her head in her hand, looking interested.

Jackson shook his head and said, "It's not a favorite of the non-Americans."

"Really? That surprises me." Hailey nodded and changed the subject. "Why sporting goods?"

He ran a hand through his hair and leaned back against the booth. "Well, the short version is that sportswear is pretty much all I knew when I graduated college. There aren't that many sporting goods stores around Sydney, and there definitely weren't places on the island I'm from. I just like the idea of providing sporting equipment to kids of all ages. Giving them the opportunity to learn about different sports and grow from them."

"Is that how you made the bulk of your wealth?" He recognized the same tone she'd used the first night when she'd been asking questions. He liked her curiosity and the way she was always thinking. He just hoped she wasn't the gold-digging type.

"No, that comes from the headset technology and other tech I've been researching."

The waiter brought out their food, and Jackson took his own opportunity to change the subject. "How did you get into real estate?"

She shrugged and stabbed a small piece of chicken with her fork. "I was good at it. Some people think you have to have a complete sales-man-type personality to thrive in real estate. But I think people just want to be heard. They want to express their ideas and have us find their dream home or a place for their growing business." She nodded toward him, and he smiled.

"You didn't want to be a doctor or lawyer or something along those lines?"

Shaking her head, she said, "No. My parents wanted me to be a nurse, but I wanted to be a social worker."

"What changed?" Jackson leaned forward, curious. He'd had plenty of interaction with social workers throughout his life, and the fact that she'd wanted to be one drew him in.

She gave him a sad smile. "I went through school for it and then was doing an internship with the city. I just…I didn't realize how hard it would be. I got too attached to the cases we worked with and couldn't move on. So I asked to leave the internship and worked to find something as far away from it as I could."

Jackson reached forward, taking her hand and giving her a reassuring smile. He wanted to say something but couldn't find the words. In the meantime, the waiter reappeared, filling their drinks again as they dug into their food. He'd think of something to say about it all later.

CHAPTER 15

Why had she never tried Indian food before? It was actually really good, but she didn't want him to know that. What was really on her mind at the moment was when his hand touched hers. He'd been through so much, had even been in the foster care system for a good portion of his life, and he hadn't judged her for not being able to hack it. She'd seen understanding in his eyes, and that was the most refreshing part.

But then again, why did his opinion matter? Life was just fine the way it was. She was happy and involved in a work she loved. Sure, she hadn't pictured herself here when she was twenty-two, but things were good. Even with the mental pep talk, she could feel that doubt and loneliness creep in just a bit, making her wonder if she was finally ready to open up and date again.

They'd eaten in silence for a few minutes when Jackson asked, "What is it about real estate that you like the most?"

"That I can make people's dreams come true, to a certain extent. I also get to use my nerdy research skills to do that." Her hand whipped to her mouth. Why had she said that?

Sure, she'd been a nerd from the time she was young, and her mind seemed to remember things even from that long ago. Those were the days when football was her favorite. She'd sit by her father while he watched a game, learning the plays, the players, and the strategies. Statistics stuck in her brain with ease, and at the age of six, most people marveled at her skills. But all that had changed when she got into college.

"I can tell you do a lot of research for your job. That's a good thing. In Brisbane, I had to switch real estate agents because the one I got just wanted to have me pay for dinner or lunch. He never came prepared with places that could be used for the store."

She studied his face and found sincerity there. It had been a while since she'd tried to put herself in someone else's shoes, but looking at him, she wondered if a lot of people tried to take advantage of him. There were plenty of people willing to suck up to get the things they wanted, and it was probably exhausting for him. "I like to be thorough. It makes me feel good when I've accomplished the job well."

He smiled, and she couldn't pull her eyes away from his strong jaw and brilliant white teeth. Taking inventory of the state of her insides, she knew she was in trouble. "That's something I learned from your father." He opened his mouth and then closed it again, as if nervous to ask her a question. Finally, he said, "I've noticed you don't particularly like football. Is there a reason?"

How could she describe all the feelings she felt connected to the sport her father had loved her whole life when a perfect stranger sat across from her? She took a few bites of food before she answered.

"There was a lot he missed out on. It was usually because he was at practice or the game or some function for your fraternity. All he did was talk about you guys, so it was hard not to feel like I didn't measure up." She looked down at her plate, unable to meet his eyes and feeling the shame of it burning her cheeks. "I don't hate it. I just wish it hadn't been such a huge part of his life for so long."

Jackson scoffed. "You think we were perfect? When he was made the head of the fraternity or the house mentor, we glued the door shut on his car so he couldn't get in."

"That was you?" Surprise wasn't a strong enough word for how she felt. "He always told us that some other football teammate had done it. Which is funny because he was just a special teams coach, not the head coach."

"That doesn't matter. What he did for us, the example he set for us, will be passed on. He may not have been the head coach, but what he did for me as a punter, helping me get stronger and kick farther, not many coaches would have done that. And then all the things he taught me about being a gentleman. Those kinds of things are priceless." He swallowed and looked at her, his eyes a little misty. "I never had a great male role model, but your dad was as close to a father as I've ever had."

Hailey felt a warm burst in her chest and was surprised to find she believed what he said. How could she not, knowing the example her father set for his kids? And from the way her mother talked about Jackson, he was practically another child anyway. He hadn't said it to get gain or to look good in her eyes. It was one of the most sincere compliments she'd ever heard.

"Thank you for saying that. He was my protector, and it's something I'm already starting to miss." She took another bite of her food, relishing the different flavors in her mouth.

"What do you think of the chicken?" he asked, wiping up the sauce on his plate with a piece of naan bread.

"It's surprisingly good. Do they have a lot of this in Australia?" Her curiosity was starting to grow as she felt herself open a little piece of the wall she'd built around her heart.

"Here and there. I've traveled quite a bit in the last few years and had to get out of my comfort zone. Believe it or not, there was a time growing up when I only ate cornflakes for breakfast, lunch, and dinner." It looked as though he tried to smile, but his face relaxed back into a natural position.

Hailey thought of one of the boys she'd worked with when she was interning as a social worker, and her stomach clenched. "Because you wanted to?"

"We didn't have much. Cornflakes were a cheap and easy meal to make. I haven't had any since I left for college and I can't even think about eating them again."

The tightening in her stomach caused a lump to form in her throat, and she did everything she could to pull back the tears. She'd had so much growing up. A father, a mother, siblings, and more food and shelter than she probably ever needed. Guilt coursed through her, and she wished she could go back and help those around her who needed help.

The check came, and she pulled out her wallet, extending a card to Jackson. He waved it away and pushed the card back to her when she tried to insist.

"This is on me. First, I am making you visit way too many properties, and then I made you try Indian food. Thank you for helping with me with this project."

"I'm glad you suggested it. I might be able to get out of my food comfort zone a bit more often." She felt the corners of her mouth turn up as she looked at him.

The waiter came back with his card, and she studied him as he bent over the receipt, writing numbers and scribbling his name. When was the last time someone voluntarily paid for her? Even Avery had made sure they alternated who took care of the bill each time. She'd thought that was just how men worked. But she'd never consciously thought about her father's actions, opening the door for her mother and always holding her hand when he had the chance.

Maybe all men weren't the same.

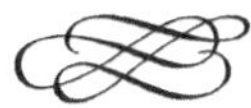

CHAPTER 16

"Should we move on to the next property?" Hailey placed her napkin onto her plate, not sure what she should say.

"I still have a few weeks left of my trip so it's not a huge rush to find something today. How about we walk around by the beach? I haven't seen it in a few days, and I think I'm going through withdrawals."

"Withdrawals? From the sand?" Hailey couldn't imagine having that problem. She liked the beach, but it wasn't her favorite place to be all the time. It was a place for lovebugs and couples. Maybe that was why she'd stayed away so long.

Jackson laughed. "Do you not have that problem? You've lived here your whole life. Are you not a go-to-the-beach-every-day kind of person?

"Not really. I've always had a lot of stuff to get done. It just seems like I come home as burned as a cherry tomato when I try to go outside and get some color."

"I promise we won't stay out that long."

They got into the car and started driving. Before long, Jackson pointed to the right. "Turn here."

Hailey frowned and said, "That's the opposite way to the beach."

"I know. I just want to see something really quick."

He gave her a few more directions, and they pulled up to a Vons grocery store.

Shifting the car into park, Hailey turned to look at Jackson, wondering what could have prompted him to come here of all places, especially since he'd just been gushing over the beach.

He turned to her, his eyes soft and said, "Do you mind if we go in for a minute? I just want to see something, well, someone."

"Uh, sure. Yeah." She pulled the keys out of the ignition and stepped out of the car. He'd been on his way to her side, but she just smiled at him, still trying to figure out what they were doing here. Was it some ex-girlfriend he wanted to reconnect with? She wished she didn't feel just a smidge jealous at the idea.

Jackson walked alongside her, which seemed odd. Avery had always just charged into places, leaving her in his wake. It felt odd to compare her ex-boyfriend to the man next to her, especially after so many years. But with the stark differences between the two, she couldn't help marveling in Jackson's overall kindness.

She moved beside him and almost jumped when she felt his hand on her lower back. She glanced at him through the corner of her eye, and his face was neutral, focused on the building in front of them.

They walked through the sliding doors and to the left by the checkout area. Jackson paused a second, his eyes searching. Once his gaze locked onto someone, a wide grin covered his face, and he strode forward.

"Janice!" he said, walking up to a woman whose gray hair had thick strips of white throughout.

She'd been standing behind a checkout stand, and she moved out to meet him. Placing a hand on each of his cheeks, she said, "Jackson Walker! What are you doing here?"

Jackson wrapped his arms around her and pulled her in for a big hug.

Hailey hung back a few steps, touched by the scene but a little confused as to who this woman was.

When he finally released her, he straightened, towering over her.

"My coach passed away, and I broke away from work to attend the funeral."

"It's so good to see you." She opened her hands and turned, as if showing him the store. "It hasn't changed too much since you left. Lots of new employees, but none like you." She paused for a moment and said, "Thank you for helping my granddaughter."

"Is she doing okay now? They got all the cancer, right?" Jackson had taken the woman's hands in his, the look on his face intense.

The woman nodded. "They did. She's got a few more months of chemo, but the doctors think she'll be in remission soon enough." Her eyes moved to Hailey, and she smiled. "I see you have a beautiful girl in your life. Girlfriend? Fiancé?"

Jackson turned to Hailey, pink tingeing his cheeks. He opened his mouth to say something, when Hailey moved forward with her hand extended.

"I'm Hailey Montgomery. Jackson came out for my dad's funeral." Her voice changed tone with the last two words, but she worked to maintain a normal expression.

The woman stepped forward and hugged Hailey, bringing the smell of jasmine to Hailey's nose. Tears threatened to spill, but Hailey pushed them back, enjoying the woman's embrace. The comfort she exuded was more than Hailey had felt in a while, aside from Jackson's embrace at the funeral. She'd avoided physical touches from her family in the past few weeks and hadn't realized how much she needed it.

"Jackson better take good care of you. Or you can always call and tell me he needs a little talking to. He has my number." Janice smiled and tilted her head down to let Hailey know she was serious.

"We're just friends, Janice. I met her for the first time when I arrived a few days ago," Jackson said, hand on his hip. The way he'd spat out friends made Hailey wonder what his true feelings were. She knew that as she found out more about his personality and his past, she was drawn to him. Did he feel the same about her?

Janice lifted a finger and said, "It doesn't matter. You should still be nice to her. You never know how things will turn out." She winked at them and stepped back into her spot behind the cash register. "Corey is still out back. He'll want to see you." Turning back to Hailey, she said, "It was so nice to meet you, my dear. I hope your family is okay."

"Thank you," was all Hailey could manage as Jackson waved to the woman and then motioned for Hailey to follow.

They walked down one of the long aisles, and she could sense an urgency and excitement in Jackson's steps as he continued forward. Once they made it to the back, Jackson pushed open the employee door, leading them into the stockroom.

She glanced around, wondering what they were doing here. He must have worked here at some point, probably in college, but she wasn't quite sure. A man on a forklift had a pallet of cardboard boxes and was moving them closer to where she and Jackson stood.

"Corey!" Jackson called, putting his hands to his mouth to amplify the sound.

The young man's head turned, and it took him a minute to recognize Jackson. Turning off the machine, he jumped down and ran to him. They hit each other's fists, bumped forearms, and then jumped to hit each other in the chest. It made her think of the celebrations in football after a touchdown.

"What are you doing here, man?" the shaggy brown-haired man said.

"Just in town for a bit. Thought I'd come by and see how things were going. Looks like you're keeping this place in shape." Jackson smiled and motioned to the room.

"I had to keep up the Jackson legacy. Who's the girl?"

Hailey now wished she'd stayed in the car. "A friend of Jackson's. How do you know him?" She may as well get some answers from these people who knew the Australian so well.

The guy, Corey, smiled. "He trained me back here when I started at sixteen. The guy can organize this place in no time. I don't think I'll ever beat his record for putting away deliveries."

Jackson slapped him on the back and said, "I'm a little rusty now."

Hailey moved to look at some pictures posted on a wall. Several looked old and faded, most of the people sporting bright yellow aprons. Right in the middle, she spotted a picture of a younger, thinner Jackson, arm wrapped around a very young Corey, and several others crowded into the picture. A faint sign read in the background, "We'll miss you!" Was this when Jackson went back to Australia?

She didn't know how long she'd been looking at the wall, but Jackson moved beside her and asked, "Are you ready?"

With a smile, she said, "Yeah."

He didn't talk as they made their way back through the store, his face thoughtful, probably thinking about his past in this place.

Once they were back in her small car, she asked, "Did you work here through college?"

His eyes were still far away, but he nodded and smiled. "When we got in trouble for messing up the hotel, the judge ordered us to pay back the damage. Most of the other guys had at least a little money to pay it off. I had nothing more than what my scholarship gave me, so your dad got me a job here. It was tough to get used to, and I felt like I was always running from one thing to another with practice and work and class, but these people became my extended family."

"And Janice's granddaughter?" Hailey had almost forgotten the small comment from Janice, but she was curious how Jackson could have helped from across the world.

He shrugged. "I try to stay in contact with people from here. There were so many who helped build a foundation for my life when I was sinking. Janice mentioned that her granddaughter had been diagnosed with a Wilms tumor, a cancer that grows on the kidney. I, uh," he shifted, looking uncomfortable all of a sudden. "I sent some money over to cover the bills. Janice doesn't make much here at the store, and the rest of her family has had a hard time."

Hailey watched as his jaw quivered slightly before he smiled, covering up the emotions. Guilt hit her in the chest. She'd judged him so quickly once she'd found out he was a billionaire, but it seemed as though he used it to help others as best as he could. She knew of people with money who'd described things like childhood cancer as being the fault of the families, looking down on their lifestyle because they were poor. It appeared that Jackson's childhood was ever present in his mind, helping to shape many of his decisions.

She locked eyes with him and said softly, "That's really cool. I can't imagine what those bills would look like." Her mom hadn't mentioned worry over bills and expenses. She wasn't sure if her parents had taken out a life insurance policy or if they'd just saved up enough over the years to not have to worry about it. Maybe she'd have to find a way to help out. If she ever found a place for Jackson's store, she'd give the commission to her mom to take care of it all.

"Ready for the beach?" Jackson asked, his face mischievous again.

"Sure." She'd be adventurous today. After these new revelations, she found herself wanting to find out more about this guy. Maybe an afternoon on the beach would help her peel back more of the layers that made up Jackson Walker.

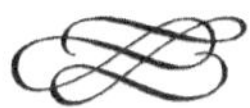

CHAPTER 17

Stopping by the grocery store had been a whim, but after seeing Janice and Corey, Jackson felt all those memories wash over him. He was grateful to the two of them and the many others who'd worked there when he'd been there. It was amazing that it took messing up like he had with the hotel rooms to help him meet some of the most influential people in his life.

Hailey drove them to a spot near Los Trancos, one of the entrances into Crystal Cove Beach. He'd only been there once, but it was still early afternoon, and only a few people sat on the sand.

Since it was January, it wasn't quite the temperature for swimming, but something about the sand between his toes seemed to clear his mind. He waited while Hailey took off her shoes and rolled her pants up to her knees.

"It's been forever since I've been here. It was one of our favorite places when I was growing up," Hailey said, her eyes half-closed as the wind whipped her hair back. "When Junior and Penny were born, this was where we spent our summers, just the sand, the water, and a lot of laughter."

They walked down to the water, and Jackson stepped onto the darker sand. "That sounds amazing. Like a fairy tale."

He held his shoes in one hand, feeling the crisp air in his lungs. The sky was overcast, but it didn't look like there was a threat of rain. This was what he'd needed after an emotional couple of days after the funeral.

"Oh, my life was no fairy tale. But I guess I can't complain too much." She paused, and he could feel her staring at him. "You mentioned you were in foster care?"

He nodded, not sure if he was ready to pull that particular box completely off the shelf. With all the questions she'd thrown at him today, it was bound to happen.

"How long were you in the system?" Her voice was soft, tender, and he turned to look at her, seeing no trace of mocking.

Blowing out a breath, he said, "About six years. My dad left before I was born. I moved with my mum several times, usually with whatever new boyfriend she had at that point. They'd be gone for a few days at a time, and when she had other babies, she'd leave them with me."

Hailey gasped, and she placed her hand on his elbow, sending fire shooting up his arm to his shoulder. He tried not to look at it resting there, hoping she wouldn't let go.

"My sister is eight years younger, and my brother is ten years younger. We'd gone through everything we could eat in the house, and my mum still hadn't come back. I knocked on the neighbor's door, asking for some food. When she came over and saw us there, she called the social workers, and we were all taken to foster care."

"Did they keep the three of you together?" He could see the worry in her face as she waited for his answer.

"The two younger ones, yes. It wasn't hard for people to take in a four-year-old and a two-year-old. But a twelve-year-old? That's a more difficult placement."

"Did you ever see them or your mom again?" Hailey asked. He wasn't sure if she'd done it on purpose, but she'd moved closer to him, the warmth of her skin filling him with a measure of comfort.

He shook his head. "No, I'd asked them to let me know when my mum came back, but they never found her. My brother and sister are both at uni, sorry, university in Australia. It took a while, but I found them about two years ago, and I see them every once in a while."

Hailey looked at him as though she wanted to ask another question but something was stopping her. Finally, she asked, "Did you move around a lot while in the system?"

Nodding, Jackson said, "I bounced around from house to house, finally staying in the last one for the last two years of school. They were good people, but I never had that feeling of family. I guess that's why your family is so special to me. I feel like I belong somewhere when I'm with them."

Positioning herself in front of him, she tilted her head back to look at him. They stood there for a moment without speaking before she reached her arms around his middle and leaned her head against his chest. More small fireworks went off inside him, and he put his arms around her lightly, reminding him of comforting her at the funeral.

When she stepped back, he saw tears in her eyes. Wiping them away with his thumb, he smiled at her. "No need to cry now. That's all in the past."

Her lips puckered, and she took a deep breath before she spoke. "My internship was with the Department of Child Services down in Anaheim, and I struggled to make it to the end of each day there. And that was your life. I don't know how you made it through all that and still ended up, well, happy and not bitter. It makes me even more grateful for my family."

"Yeah, your family is pretty great." They started walking, but this time, the couple of inches between them felt like too much distance to Jackson.

"Should we go look at the property near here? They said they couldn't meet after three today." Hailey looked at him, her business face back in place. As much as he didn't feel like looking at more properties today, he didn't want to go back to the Montgomery house just yet. He wasn't quite sure what he was feeling for the firecracker daughter of his coach, but it was escalating at a rate that scared him.

With all he'd learned about her today, he knew there was something deeper that held her back from doing a lot of things. She was stubborn, but she was also kind and sympathetic, and she made his blood pressure rise with every touch. He felt like the connection between them had tripled, and he began to wonder if a relationship between the two of them just might work.

fter the beach, Hailey had taken him to a property that had a lot of good points to it, but it was smaller than he wanted it to be, and the price was a bit higher than he'd figured in his numbers. Sure, he could afford to pay the extra, but he didn't want to sink the project before it even had a chance to thrive.

Walking into the Montgomery house, he smelled shrimp and smiled. As he turned to Hailey, she scrunched up her nose. "Ugh. Is that seafood?"

He nodded and smiled at her. She just responded by rolling her eyes. Walking into the kitchen, they found that Penny had already set the table and was bringing over condiments for what looked like shrimp tacos.

"This smells amazing, Penny," he said, glancing over at Hailey.

Clenching her teeth, Hailey said, "Yeah. Great."

Penny grinned and moved back for another bowl.

Jackson nudged Hailey. He leaned down and said, "You just tried Indian food today. Give it a chance. You might even like it."

She tried to look angry and punched him on the shoulder, causing him to chuckle.

Mrs. M. walked into the kitchen and looked between the two of them. "What did I miss?"

He draped his arm around Hailey's shoulders and wiggled his eyebrows at her. "We're working on developing Hailey's taste buds."

"I'd love to see that. This girl is the pickiest eater I've ever seen." Mrs. M. folded her arms against her chest and leaned back against the island.

Jackson dropped his arm, watching the fire in Hailey's eyes grow. "Well, Mom, I ate buttery chicken today." She'd tilted her chin up and tried to look victorious.

In a loud whisper, he said, "Butter chicken. Indian food."

"You got her into a place with food from another country? Jackson, you must teach me your ways." Mrs. M. laughed, and Hailey frowned, her eyes almost closed as she tried to stare at her mom.

"Sit down. I'll run and get Junior." Penny motioned for them to sit at the table.

Jackson took his spot from the times before, catching Hailey's eye as he sat down.

"Jackson told me last night you were helping him find property, Hailey. Were you able to find anything for your store today, Jackson?" Mrs. M. asked.

"Not quite," Jackson said, shaking his head and pulling his lips in.

"Yeah, Mr. Picky Pants over here," Hailey said, grinning at Jackson, "thinks he needs something a little bigger or a little smaller, depending on what we were looking at right then." She giggled, and Jackson laughed at her joke. It was nice that she had relaxed a little bit since the first time he'd met her. It made her even more likeable. And attractive. Her real smile lit up her whole face, causing the green in her eyes to pop a bit more.

"So, what's the plan for tomorrow?" Mrs. M. looked between the two of them, waiting for an answer.

Hailey leaned forward on the table. "Well, since it'll be Saturday, we should do something fun. Get out of the house or something. That was always the best day with Dad during the offseason. I think he'd like it if we had some fun."

Mrs. M. turned to Jackson and asked, "What haven't you done in a while? Or what did you not have a chance to do while you were here in college?"

Jackson brought his hand to his chin, trying to think about what was around Anaheim Hills and what he had always wanted to do.

"That's a good question. We didn't really do much outside of frat activities and the occasional trip to the beach. So I'm up for whatever you guys want to do." When Jackson saw Hailey's smirk, he wondered what he'd just gotten himself into.

Penny came downstairs with Junior following close behind. After a quick prayer to bless the food, they dished out their shrimp tacos.

"What did I miss?" Penny looked around at them, waiting for an answer.

"Oh, nothing. We're just trying to find something to do with Jackson tomorrow," Mrs. M. said.

"Disneyland!" Penny's eyes grew wide, and she was practically hopping in her seat.

Four pairs of eyes turned to Jackson, and Junior asked, "Have you ever been to Disneyland?"

Jackson shook his head. "It always sounded fun, I just never had the money to go. Aren't we a little old to go there?"

The Montgomerys laughed, and Hailey said, "You thought I was boring. Wait until you see me at Disneyland. That will change your mind."

"But will it be crowded on a Saturday?" He shifted in his seat, not wanting to think about being stuck in the middle of hundreds of people.

"It might be, but you're not afraid of crowds, are you?" Hailey's grin pulled him in, and he gave her a reluctant smile.

"No, but from what I've heard, there are a lot of people there. More than Hawthorne's football stadium. Having to weave in and out of that many people…I'd have Buckley's chance of surviving."

"Buckley's what?" Penny asked, a deep crease in her forehead.

Jackson looked around at them for a few seconds with his mouth open, registering it was another Aussie thing. "It just means there isn't a chance."

Hailey cocked her head to the side. "This coming from the guy who gave me a hard time about not wanting to try different cuisine?" She scrunched her nose at him, causing him to chuckle. "Well, we can leave whenever you want. But they have a lot of fun rides. And some amazing food to try."

They'd all served themselves food by then, and a silence descended upon them as they began to eat. The conversation moved on to something else shortly after, but Jackson kept thinking about the American amusement park. He'd never thought too much about it in college, knowing he couldn't go to the park and pay rent in the same month, even with the low price of frat housing.

An excitement started to swirl inside. Even now, after years of building his own business, his life still amazed him sometimes, that he had the money to pay for things like an amusement park or to fly across the world first class. And if the girl sitting to his left was going to be there, tomorrow would be a day to remember.

CHAPTER 19

*H*ailey woke up early, every bit of her excited to ride the rides and enjoy the food at one of her favorite places. Her dad had never been a huge fan of anywhere with crowds, but she'd gone several times with school groups and friends. Every time seemed as magical as the last, even after she'd walked for hours and was ready to sleep for days.

For some reason, she was even more excited to share this with Jackson. They'd shared a moment yesterday, one revealing a vulnerability that Avery wouldn't have shared even after dating for three years. Her negative thoughts about rich people were going from a generalization to those selected few people from memory who had soured her toward wealth, and she was grateful for that.

What he'd been through had defined him, but it hadn't made him bitter against the world. Maybe he had been at one point, but life had a way of smoothing out the rough edges if a person let it.

Dressed in some shorts and a Disney t-shirt, she walked out of her old bedroom. She'd decided to stay at her mom's house the night before, playing games and eating snacks until much later than they should have. But she knew she'd need to get everyone going this morning if they were going to make it in line before the gates opened.

She jumped when she saw Jackson on the landing. "What are you doing up already?"

"I guess I'm still a little mixed up on time zones. I've been awake since four." He rubbed his hands over his face and looked at her with heavy lids.

Hailey pulled out her phone and checked to see that it was only six thirty in the morning. "That's not fun," she said. "Hopefully you can power through because I'm planning on staying late. Are you ready to go?"

"You said we could leave whenever I want." He smiled at her, a little apprehensive.

"That's because we were at the table. You've survived tougher practices with my dad than just walking around a park all day. You'll be fine." She smacked her hand across his chest, surprised that it was so firm.

"You're the expert, but this better not be some kind of hazing ritual to first-time Disney goers. It might make me avoid the place forever." His voice raised along with his eyebrows.

Moving in a little closer, she got a whiff of his cologne again, the woodsy scent making her long for the camping trips they used to go on as a family. Shaking herself out of those thoughts, she said, "You'll be fine. We will be there to guide you." She walked forward, moving her feet quickly down the stairs.

"That's what I'm worried about," Jackson called after her, taking the steps at a slower pace. "Just don't leave me somewhere all by myself."

Hailey chuckled, and Jackson's shoulders tensed even more. "We won't leave you. My mom would kill us if we did." Her words must have calmed him, because he blew out a long breath.

"Then I'd better stay right by Mrs. M. She'll make sure I'm protected." He grinned, and something passed between them, causing Hailey's smile to falter.

Moving a little bit, she felt a shiver go down her spine. She turned, glancing over her shoulder before walking into the kitchen. "I don't think you'll have a problem with defending yourself. You're at least six inches taller than me, so you're about six feet, two inches tall, and I bet you weigh close to two-twenty."

Jackson frowned. "It's been a while since I've had to do the math conversions, so I'll just pretend you're right and make my morning easier."

Hailey laughed at that, having forgotten about the different measurement systems in Australia. What would it have been like to come to school in the States and have to relearn the measurements here?

Opening a cupboard, she pulled out a bowl and poured in some shredded wheat, adding milk until the squares were almost covered.

"That's a lot of milk," Jackson said, giving her a side-glance.

"Yeah, but it makes the cereal nice and soft so I don't feel like I'm breaking a tooth."

Jackson pulled out a bagel and popped it in the toaster sitting on the counter. "That's the beauty of a bagel. As long as you don't burn it, it will be mostly soft."

Her mind recalled their discussion about his childhood from the day before, and she wondered if he even ate cereal anymore. She couldn't blame him if he didn't.

"What time are we leaving?" Jackson's deep voice seemed to pulse through her chest. It was such a strange feeling, like opening up a section of herself she hadn't felt in a long time.

"The park opens at eight this morning, so if we don't hear my family getting up in the next fifteen minutes or so, we'll have to go wake them up."

"We're going right when it opens?" The hesitation on his face caused her to chuckle.

She tried to give him a serious look but ended up smiling more. "You're the one who's worried about crowds. If we go right when it opens, we'll be able to get on all the rides fairly quickly. Most of the people start showing up just before or after lunch."

Jackson didn't look like he believed her, but she didn't blame him. Getting there early was something she'd learned from her dad. If she got up early enough to run errands, they took half as long as when she went later in the day. Disneyland was no exception.

A few minutes later, her mom walked into the kitchen, yawning as she walked over to the fridge. "Are we sure about this? I felt like I slept a total of two hours last night, thanks to you game bugs. I should've gone to bed right after that first game of Skip-Bo."

Hailey gave her mom a sympathetic look and went back to eating the last few squares of her cereal. "We can always take two cars in case some of us need to come back early," she volunteered.

Her mom looked at her and then nodded. "I can live with that. We might have to have a second car if the other two don't wake up soon."

Jackson took his bagel out of the toaster and smeared cream cheese and then jelly on top. He moved to sit on a stool next to Hailey at the island. When she scrunched her nose at his bagel, he said, "I learned it from Evan in college. I thought the combination would be crazy, but I rather enjoy it."

"To each his own, I guess," Hailey said.

Soon enough, Penny and Junior came walking in, both dressed for the day while rubbing their eyes.

"Can't we go in the afternoon like normal people?" Junior asked, his eyes only open a slit.

Hailey stood to take her bowl to the sink. "We were just talking about taking two cars. If you want to wait, you can, but I'm not saving spots for you."

Junior made a face, pretending to mock her, making Hailey grin even wider. He stopped and pulled another box of cereal from the pantry.

After everyone was fed, they had piled into her mom's crossover and Hailey's compact car by ten to seven and were driving the distance to Disneyland. They parked in one of the outer lots, then hopped on one of the shuttles, arriving at the gates by 7:30 a.m.

"Hailey, why don't you go help Jackson get his ticket, and we'll stand in line by the gates. Just come find us when you're through," her mom said.

Hailey was grateful her mother hadn't given her some ridiculous teasing face, even though she knew her mom was trying to push them together as much as possible. A few days ago, she would have been annoyed, but now, after getting to know Jackson a little more yesterday, she didn't actually mind.

She went to grab his arm but grabbed his hand by accident and pulled him toward the little round kiosks in the middle of Disneyland and California Adventure Parks.

"You all don't need to get tickets?" He motioned to where the rest of her family had disappeared.

Shaking her head, Hailey said, "No, we have yearly passes. I convinced my mom to get them when we brought my dad." Studying his face, she asked, "Are you excited?"

He shrugged his shoulders and said, "I guess. I don't really know what to expect."

"Did you ever have a favorite Disney movie growing up?"

"I like *The Lion King*. There weren't a whole lot of movies in our house as a kid. I remember seeing a few in some of the foster homes I lived in, but by that time, I wasn't really interested in cartoons."

"So, what you're trying to say is that you're a long-lost king who's finally come back to his kingdom?" She giggled a little at the thought, but when she saw the serious expression on his face, she replayed the words in her mind and realized just how close she'd come with that answer. He might not have been born into his social class, but he'd certainly made something of himself.

"What's your favorite movie?" he asked her.

"I've always been a fan of *Sleeping Beauty*, but I really like the new Rapunzel, *Tangled*."

The ticket agent was waiting for them, and after a few minutes and an exchange of a credit card, they had a ticket. People were already moving through the gates and they had to look around for her family once the attendant scanned their tickets.

"I thought you said it didn't open until eight," Jackson said, looking at his watch. "Did your family already go through?"

Hailey bit her bottom lip. "It doesn't. They just let you through a little early, and then you can wait up closer to the rides." She pulled out a map she'd picked up at the kiosk and started pointing out the rides. "Where do you want to start?"

Jackson blew out a long breath, swiping his hand through his hair as he glanced between the crowd and the map. "I'll let you be the tour guide today."

"Let's go find the others and we'll make a plan from there."

CHAPTER 20

The day had been long but good, and Jackson was surprised by how much fun he had. They rode on just about every ride, even most of the kiddie rides. Penny had dragged him to meet several of the characters they'd come across, and it was like a dream from his childhood. And Hailey had lied. There was no way his feet had ever hurt this much after a practice with Coach.

The sky was almost dark, and it was just Jackson and Hailey together. Penny and Junior had found some friends from school and moved off to other parts of the park, and Mrs. M. had decided to go home around four, complaining of a headache.

Jackson was sure he was going to feel awkward with just Hailey around, but she'd been so carefree and fun, showing a completely different side of her than when they first met.

"We should probably go get our spots for the light show," Hailey said.

"Already? It's not supposed to be for another hour, right?" Jackson frowned. He felt like he'd finally gotten a handle on all of the Max Pass stuff that allowed them to get on the rides faster than standing in the longer lines. He could understand being early to things, but waiting an hour for a light show was a new experience.

With a light laugh, she said, "We have the pass for it, but we still have to get a spot. We can go up by the fence and just sit while we wait."

As they waited, they talked about things here and there, about work and what it was like living in Australia. Then they heard the fountains go off, and Hailey sat up, helping to pull him up. She clapped in excitement, and at that moment, Jackson wondered if she had really grown up. He smiled wide as he watched her stare out at the pictures broadcast on the water. The soft curls of her hair hung over one shoulder, and it took some doing to look away.

The show was impressive, with the coordinated lights and video along with the music. At one point, the water splashed up and got them wet. Within minutes, Hailey had moved closer to his side, shivering.

Jackson didn't have anything to wrap around her. He draped his arm over her shoulders and brought her closer to him, and she turned so her arms were pressed into his abdomen. He could smell vanilla in her hair, and he took in a deep breath, wanting to savor the moment.

He wasn't sure when he'd started to fall for Hailey Montgomery, but he'd never felt like this with any other girl he'd dated. Her confidence and spunk made her attractive, but her willingness to listen made her someone he could trust. And he hadn't had that since...well, since her father was alive.

At one point, she started shivering so much that he moved his lips near her ear so she could hear him. "Do you want to go?"

She pulled back and looked up at him.

Their eyes locked for several seconds, the tension between them thickening, and he couldn't fight the draw of her lips.

Leaning in, he touched his lips to hers, soft at first, as if testing. When he felt her lean in, he deepened the kiss, pulling her tighter to him.

After a few seconds, he pulled away, looking into her eyes with a smile on his lips.

She smiled at him and glanced down, not breaking his grip around her. "Let's go. I'm freezing, and it will be nice to beat the crowds." She only looked up long enough for him to nod.

Jackson stepped in front of her, taking her hand in his and moving through the crowd. He liked the feel of it in his, smaller but not so small that he felt as if he could crush it.

When they made it through the crowd and out to the slight slope leading to the exit, Jackson glanced over and was entranced by the look on Hailey's face. Her eyes were beaming, and the way she bit her lower lip made his heart beat just a bit faster.

"Thanks for today. It's something I'll never forget." He smiled, and she grinned at him.

"I'm glad you came. It was a lot of fun. I'll never forget your face after Splash Mountain." She giggled, and Jackson poked her in the side, causing her to jump away quickly. "Hey! Not fair."

He pulled her arm around his lower back and draped his arm over her shoulder as they walked out to catch the shuttle.

"Wait. Don't we need to find your brother and sister?" Jackson looked down at her and raised an eyebrow.

Hailey pulled out her phone and clicked on her messages. After a few seconds, she said, "I guess not. Penny already left, and Junior is getting a ride home with his friend Ashley."

Jackson wiggled his eyebrows. "Ashley, huh?"

Her laugh sounded airy, and Jackson could listen to it the rest of the night and be happy. "They've been friends for a long time. But she's a good girl. She definitely fits with him."

Jackson paused a second before he asked, "And what about us?"

"What about us?"

"Do you think we fit?"

$\mathcal{H}$ailey could feel her heart pounding against her ribcage. The bus opened its doors at that moment, giving her a second to think about Jackson's question.

Once they sat down, she turned to look at him. One corner of his mouth turned up, but she saw a hint of worry in his eyes.

"I think we've got potential." As she turned to look ahead, Jackson reached over and interlaced his fingers with hers. She squeezed his hand a moment, sure this was all a dream. It had been a while since she'd been kissed, and with the light show going on in the background, she was sure the fireworks had been set off earlier than normal. She could still feel the buzz in her lips.

They rode the bus to the parking lot in a comfortable silence. On the drive to her mother's home, they took turns choosing songs on the radio, belting them out at the top of their lungs. Hailey's favorite part was the way Jackson would substitute similar-sounding words when he didn't know them exactly.

When she turned onto the street of her parents' home, she glanced at Jackson, and excitement bubbled up in her. She didn't know what was going on or if there was a future with him, but for now, the night was enough.

Jackson opened the front door for her, and they walked in.

"I'm not really tired. Are you?" she asked, taking a step closer to him.

He shook his head, his eyes wider than she'd seen before.

"Movie and popcorn?"

"Yeah, I need to change first. My shirt is still wet." Jackson held out his shirt, and it was stuck to his abs. She had to consciously keep her teeth clenched so she wouldn't look like some drooling idiot.

"Okay, we'll both change, and then come back and watch a movie. First one down gets to pick." She winked at him and bolted up the stairs, hearing his steps right behind her.

"Challenge accepted." He ducked into the room he was staying in while she took the next few feet at a leap.

Pulling open her old dresser drawer, she found a pair of taco pajama pants and a t-shirt that said, "Readers gonna read." It would have to do.

After pulling on the clothes, she grabbed a hair tie from the night-stand before rushing out the door. She felt her adrenaline surge as she hurried past Jackson's door and started down the stairs.

His door opened, and she moved her feet faster down the familiar steps, not ready to relinquish the choice of movie to him. She had no idea if he was an action-and-adventure-only guy, but she was going to test that with a chick flick.

She moved into the kitchen and pulled a bag of microwave popcorn out of the cupboard. Pulling off the plastic, she set it into the microwave and pushed start.

"I wasn't expecting you to be so fast." Jackson's accent sounded thicker this late at night, probably from the exhaustion of a long day. She noticed the definition of his legs as she glanced at the long green basketball shorts he was wearing, and the gray t-shirt fit him snugly, causing her pulse to jump again.

Focusing on a comeback, she said, "I may be a bit competitive." She leaned a hand on the counter and looked up at him.

Man, those eyes were gorgeous.

He moved to mirror her pose. "Competitive, huh? Why does that not surprise me?" He gave her a lopsided grin, and she giggled. He'd turned her back into a teenager.

A door opened, and her mother came into the kitchen. "How was it? Everything you thought it would be?"

Jackson smiled at her, nodding. He turned his gaze back to Hailey and said, "Definitely."

Hailey's breath caught in her throat, and she coughed, walking over to the sink to fill a cup with water.

"How's your headache, Mrs. M.?"

Hailey turned around, to see Jackson leaned against the counter, arms folded against his chest. How much did he work out? Because those were definitely not the arms of a punter.

"Feeling better. I think I'll just turn in and hope I don't get sick." She looked between Hailey and Jackson and with raised eyebrows, said, "Don't stay up too late, ya hear?"

"We'll be fine, Mom. Believe it or not, we are adults now."

"But you'll always be my kids." She grinned at them, and Jackson's face went slack. Her mom waved to them just as the microwave beeped.

Hailey pulled the popcorn out and moved in the direction of the family room. "Are you ready?"

It took Jackson a minute to respond, as if he'd been stuck inside his head. He turned and followed her.

"Grab a blanket and take a seat on the couch." She poured the popcorn into a larger bowl and set it on the coffee table. "I'll get the movie started. Are there any genres you don't really like?"

Jackson shrugged, there but not mentally present.

Hailey shrugged it off, turning back to the wall of movies stacked on built-in shelving. She pulled out one of her favorite movies and stuck it in the Blu-ray player.

Taking a seat next to Jackson, she pulled the blanket from the basket next to the sofa. She flicked it over her legs and didn't think to ask before sharing it with him, resting it over his lower body as well. She pushed play and pulled the popcorn bowl closer, setting it in between them. Throwing a few kernels into her mouth, she pushed the button to fast-forward through the previews.

"So, what is it we're watching?" Jackson asked, his eyes clear and his demeanor back to normal. He threw a few popcorn kernels into his mouth and chewed, looking at her with those crystal-blue eyes.

Cue the swoon.

"It's called *Return to Me.* I figured you might not like the ultra-sappy movies, so I thought I'd play one that has a lot of laughs in it. Well, around the middle."

"What do you mean 'around the middle'? Are you saying I'm going to cry?" Jackson made a pouting face, causing Hailey to laugh.

When he didn't smile, she narrowed her eyes, trying to decide if he was being serious or joking. "Do you really cry during movies?"

He gave her a sheepish grin and nodded. "Maybe."

She sat back, stunned. To find a guy who cried was rare, but to find one who admitted to it? Well, she'd never met one until now.

The movie started playing, and after a few minutes, Hailey scooted closer, laying her head on his shoulder. She was debating whether it was a good move or not, as she wasn't used to being so forward. But since he'd kissed her at the park and had held her hand a few times throughout the day, she didn't think this was too much. She glanced up at him to see the same vacant expression as before. What could he be thinking about?

She must have fallen asleep some time later, because she woke up in Jackson's arms as he tried to open her bedroom door.

"I'm so sorry," she said as her head lay against his shoulder. "I didn't even realize I fell asleep."

He grinned, showing just how tired he was by the dark circles under his eyes. "Want to know a secret? I fell asleep too. I heard the music at the end of the movie and figured it was time for both of us to get some real sleep."

She dropped one leg, so he let her down. A surge of heat rushed up her neck as she looked at him. "Thank you for bringing me upstairs." There was an awkward silence for a few moments, and then she said, "I'll see you in the morning?"

"Of course. Maybe we should take a day to rest instead of running all over Southern California." He ran his thumb over her jaw for a moment and moved away, leaving her with that lopsided grin.

Once the door was closed, Hailey threw herself down on the bed and sighed. She was in big trouble. Her heart was telling her she was on the brink of falling for the Australian billionaire, and for the first time in a long time, her brain agreed.

CHAPTER 22

The next morning, Hailey woke up late and found that most of the family was already going about their day. Her mother was out pulling a few weeds in the garden, and Penny had slept over at a friend's house.

Bringing a bagel with cream cheese outside, Hailey sat next to her mother and chewed a bite, trying to wake up. "Where are Junior and Jackson?" She tried to make the question seem nonchalant, even though inside she was more than curious.

"Jackson went with Junior to play some basketball with his friends. Junior was pretty excited." Her mom leaned forward, using clippers to trim a section of dead bush.

"I bet. Basketball is his world, and it seems he's always had a good relationship with Jackson." She wasn't really sure if the last statement was correct since she'd avoided him all those years ago. Part of her just wanted to hear more about Jackson.

She laughed inwardly at the change in direction her feelings had made. A week ago, she would tune out any story that contained Jackson Walker. Now her curiosity urged her to learn all she could, her mind going to the amazing kiss they'd shared the night before.

"Jackson has always been good with Junior, and your brother has idolized him to a certain degree. What I want to know is what is your current relationship with Jackson?" Her mother gave her a quick grin before throwing the dead branch onto a pile on the sidewalk.

Hailey sighed and took a large bite of her bagel, chewing to allow her time to think. "He's a good guy, Mom. I mean, I wanted to hate him because he was a football player and Dad's golden boy, but he's so nice and kind and sweet. It's no wonder you guys always talked about him." She paused again and then said, "He kissed me."

She said it softly, but her mother turned quickly, her eyes narrowing to scrutinize Hailey's face. This wasn't the first time Hailey had wondered if her mom had the hearing of a dog.

"And?"

Hailey flopped back onto the somewhat-dry winter grass and looked up at the wisps of clouds in the sky. "It was amazing. My lips still feel like they're on fire."

Her mother chuckled. "That's always a good sign. When did he kiss you?"

"Toward the end of the light show. It was like straight out of a fairy tale." Hailey touched her fingers to her lips, remembering the sound of the water in the background.

She turned and saw her mom raise an eyebrow. "So, no kissing on the couch last night?" she asked.

Hailey sat up and wanted to cringe as she admitted, "We both fell asleep. He tried to carry me to bed, though, which was adorable."

"And your feelings about him are…?"

What was with all of the questions today? But Hailey found that she didn't mind as she wanted to gush about everything all of a sudden.

"I really like him. Sure, I've only known him for a week, but I hope it lasts another week and then another." She put the last piece of her bagel in her mouth and wrapped her arms around her knees, pulling them in to her chest.

"Well, just make sure you don't break his heart. He's a sweet boy, and he's been through a lot." Her mother gave her that no-nonsense look she was so good at.

Irritation webbed its way through her stomach. "What do you mean I shouldn't break his heart?" She tried to keep the malice out of her words, but she had to say the last few words with her teeth clenched.

"I'm just saying that if at some point you aren't interested in him, let him know before leading him on."

Standing, Hailey put a hand on her hip and said, "I'm your daughter, Mom. Don't you think you should be on my side?"

"I am on your side, honey. But Jackson means a lot to this family too."

"It doesn't sound like it. Just because I haven't had a relationship in a long time doesn't mean I'm the one hurting all the guys I've gone on a date with. And my last boyfriend gave me a concussion because I didn't have enough money to pay off his gambling debt. So forgive me if I don't get your meaning, Mom." Marching back into the house, Hailey didn't look back at her mother as she kept calling her name.

It was just like her mom to side with a football player. Her thoughts started spinning, and she ran up to her room, tears falling before she hit the pillow. She wanted to be mad at Jackson, but with everything that had happened the past couple of days, she knew she couldn't be mad at him. He hadn't done anything to cause her mother's comment.

A knock sounded at the door, and Hailey did her best to ignore it. She heard the squeak and her mother's soft footfalls get closer to the bed. The bed sank a bit, and then Hailey felt her mother's fingers combing through her hair.

"I'm sorry, honey. I didn't think before I spoke. It's been so long that I'd almost forgotten about Avery."

Sniffing, Hailey looked up at her through hazy eyes. "But I haven't, Mom. Sure, I've been able to work through it, and I'm in a much better place than I was years ago, but when it comes to getting into a relationship, I'm not taking it lightly ever again."

"I know. Just don't shut Jackson out because he was an athlete and he has money. That's about the only similarities he has to Avery, remember that."

Hailey nodded, finally realizing her mother was right. "That's true. It's just that this is the first time I'm actually excited about a guy again. I only hope it doesn't turn out like the last time."

Her mother continued to comb her fingers through Hailey's hair, helping her to relax somewhat. "It won't, honey. But trust your instincts, good or bad."

Chewing on the side of her mouth, Hailey nodded. That was the only thing she could do.

CHAPTER 23

It had been good to spend the day with Junior and even better to work out some of the stiffness from walking around Disneyland. Jackson had come back to find Hailey gone but was happy once she texted, saying she'd just gone home to work on a few things so they'd have other properties to look at the next day.

He reflected on the near perfect weekend, the highlights playing in his mind. The kiss, the movie, and then carrying Hailey to her room all made him smile as he thought about them. His brain told him to go for it, to see if a relationship between the two of them could work out.

Something in him hesitated, and the memory of Mrs. M. saying Jackson would always be her child caused him to freeze. Jackson had been worried about a long-distance relationship with anyone, since he lived so far away, but as he thought more about a relationship with Hailey, he drew back, worried that it would ruin his relationship with the rest of the Montgomerys if things didn't work out with her long-term. He'd hardly been able to concentrate on the movie because he was so focused on the internal debate.

When Monday morning hit, Jackson sat at the kitchen island with some scrambled eggs and toast in front of him. It was about the only thing he could cook, and it was a nice break from bagels. He took a bite of his toast, hearing the front door open as he did.

Shoes clicked against the tile in the hallway, and Hailey walked into the kitchen, dressed in dark slacks and a red long-sleeved blouse. Her hair fell in waves over her shoulders, and she looked beautiful for so early in the morning.

"Good morning," she said with a smile, walking over and popping two pieces of bread in the toaster. Turning back to him, she said, "I forgot to eat before I left my house. Your toast looks good."

"It is good because I made it," he said, winking at her.

Color blossomed on her cheeks, and she moved to lean on the counter in front of him. "Are we ready to get back on the hunt for your dream property?" She laughed as she said it, and Jackson couldn't help but join in. He liked that quirky sense of humor and the fact that she laughed at her own jokes.

"Where are we off to today?"

"Not the beach, sadly. We've got a couple of properties to look at just north of Anaheim Hills and then one to the south. Which direction would you like to go first?" She glanced up at him, and he couldn't pull his eyes from her face.

When he realized she was giving him a crazy face, sticking out her tongue and crossing her eyes at him, he laughed. "You're too chipper for this early in the morning."

"This coming from the guy who still gets up super early every morning." She raised her eyebrow, as if issuing a challenge.

"I actually slept until seven thirty this morning, which is almost a miracle." He took a drink of the milk in the small glass in front of him. "Let's try the north ones. If there's more than one, maybe we can find something that will work. I'm still partial to the old bookstore, though."

Hailey grinned, and it felt like sparks from a firecracker going off in his chest. "Really? That could be a good spot. Central location."

"That's what I was thinking. But let's see these others and decide after." He rinsed off his plate and set it in the dishwasher, not wanting to make any more work for Mrs. M. She'd been so tired the last few days, and he hoped she wasn't getting sick.

He grabbed his wallet and phone, slipping them into his pockets, and Hailey led the way out the door, typing something furiously into her phone. When they got near the car, she turned to him. "Do you want to drive? It will make it easier for me to get all the facts for the properties before we see them."

"Sure."

Jackson got behind the wheel of her small sedan, his knee hitting the dashboard. He bit his lower lip, hoping to focus on that rather than the pain until it subsided. He pulled on the lever, scooting the chair back into a more comfortable position for his legs. He had to focus more, just like driving to the funeral, since the steering wheel was in the left side of the car. Everything was backward compared to Australia, and while he'd driven in plenty of places with the cars on the other side of the road, the first few minutes took extra concentration.

"You tell me where I need to go." He pulled out of the driveway and down the street, stopping at a stoplight. "How was your day yesterday? I didn't get to see you much."

Hailey's eyes didn't meet his, almost like she was avoiding him. "It was good. I just relaxed at my apartment and looked through some more listings. How was playing with Junior?" She looked up now, eager to hear his answer.

"It was really good. Junior's got a lot of good friends, and I think they're helping him get through all this." He watched as she swallowed and nodded.

"That's good. I always worry about him, especially since he's so quiet. I just wish I could connect with him about basketball, but that wasn't one of the sports I grew up learning about." She turned her eyes back to the papers and her phone.

Jackson moved his jaw back and forth, trying to decide if he wanted to ask her the question that had plagued him for the last week. "I still don't get why you don't like football."

"Where do I even start? Honestly, I didn't start to hate it until I went to college. It seemed like all my dad did was focus on football and then the frat house. I know it was his job and whatnot, but there was always a part of me that was jealous, always wondering if the boys would know my father better than I did." She adjusted how she sat in the passenger seat, crossing her legs over each other.

"What made you think that?" Jackson asked, trying to keep his eyes on the road instead of straying toward her face.

"Well, it's sad to say, but it was mostly your fault. Well—"

"My fault?" Jackson cut her off and jabbed his hand into his chest. "I moved back to Australia after graduation and have only been back a few times to visit. And you're still blaming me?"

Hailey held up her hands and said, "Hold on. Just relax. This was before I knew you. It just felt like all my dad ever did was talk about how great you were and all the things you were accomplishing. I just didn't feel like I measured up to his expectations." She took a breath and then looked at him with glassy eyes. "And then, when I decided to be a real estate agent, he acted as though I was passing up my calling in life."

"Am I hearing you right? You think your dad didn't know every-thing that was going on in your life?" He glanced at Hailey, who nodded at him. "Well, let me just tell you that it was me who never thought I met Coach's expectations. I always screwed up one way or another, and then I'd have to see that disappointment on his face. Sometimes the fear of that look pushed me away from doing some-thing wrong."

"That makes me feel a little bit better," Hailey said with a hint of a smile.

Jackson grinned. "Well, it better. Your father loved you, and we all knew it. Do you know how many times I've been compared to you? He'd use examples from your life to show us that we needed to shape up or we'd never find the girl for us."

A reddish color tinted her cheeks, and Jackson smiled even wider. "That sounds really weird when I say it like that, right?"

She nodded emphatically and said, "Wouldn't that make you feel weird? People I don't know learned all about the mistakes I made in my life."

"If you made a mistake, we never heard about it. The examples were always successes." Jackson shrugged. "I think it would be weird to know that your father wanted us to find someone similar to you. But that should also be a great compliment, don't you think?"

She opened and closed her mouth several times before telling him to turn right. They pulled in front of a large space, and it looked nice from the outside. But it was what was inside that would make all the difference in his decision.

And everything he'd learned about Hailey told him that he'd be lucky to find someone as great as her ever again. The thought scared him a bit and he just hoped he wouldn't screw it all up. He had fallen hard and fast for the Coach's daughter.

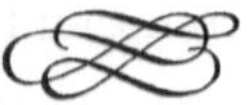

CHAPTER 24

*A*fter spending the day with Hailey, Jackson was a little worried he'd scared her. He was still a stranger in a lot of ways, but her father's stories made him feel as though he knew the girl sitting next to him.

She had smiled and laughed in the appropriate places and had done a lot of good descriptions of the places they looked at, but there was something off in her demeanor. He still felt the explosion of sparks when they touched, which was a good sign. He held her hand a couple of times, which only increased those sensations, but he could sense there was still something deeper that was bugging her.

He spent all of Tuesday curled up in the guest room he'd been staying in, answering emails and participating in conference calls. The business was running well, even with him gone, which told him that he'd hired the right people. After a few phone calls, he had several companies ready to get products created once he'd found a place for his store.

Running his fingers through his short hair, he took a breath, feeling the exhaustion from getting up early enough to communicate with Australia.

A knock sounded on the door, causing Jackson to sit up.

"Come in," he said. His heart started beating at a frantic pace in the hopes that Hailey was on the other side of the door. But in walked Penny instead.

"Do you want to come play a game?" she asked.

"Sure," Jackson said, looking at the mess of papers and his computer strewn across his bed. "Give me ten minutes, and I'll be down."

"Yes! I'm so excited. You beat me the other night, but I'm here for revenge. I didn't realize how much I've missed our bantering sessions." Penny practically hopped out the door.

Jackson shook his head and chuckled. She had so much energy, and after the long week, he felt drained.

He cleaned up his paperwork and set his laptop on the nightstand. Glancing in the mirror, he drew a comb through his hair, adding a little bit of his hair cream to make him look presentable. He pulled out a polo shirt, which was nicer than the t-shirt he'd been hanging out in most of the day. Before heading down, he breathed into his hand and turned toward the bathroom instead. With time to only grab a sandwich and head back upstairs around lunch time, he hadn't had much opportunity to do anything else.

Coming down the stairs, he found Penny with a card game on the table. UNO.

He was going to dominate. It brought back so many memories of card and board games at the Montgomery house. When was the last time he'd even had time to play a game before this trip? He smiled at Penny, and she wiggled her pointer finger at him, most likely reading his face.

"I've been practicing since the last time you were here, and I remember all your tricks. So watch out!" She took a seat across the table and dealt out three piles.

"Who else is playing?"

"My mom said she wanted to." Penny arranged the draw pile in the middle of the table.

He cleared his throat and then asked, "Awesome. Where are Junior and Hailey?"

"Junior had an after-school thing, and Hailey said she was going to be by a little later. I don't know what she's working on, because she's only supposed to be working on finding your store property."

That made Jackson pause a moment. She *had* sort of admitted she only had him as a client at the moment that first day in her office. As he thought about Hailey, he realized he hadn't seen or heard from her all day. Not that they were at the stage where they had to communicate all the time, but it left him with a hollow feeling, confirming his feelings from the day before that something was off between them. Did he say or do something to bug her?

Mrs. M. walked in and sat down. "Who's ready to get beat?" she said, giving them a fake glare. She'd never been good at the intimidation factor, but Jackson loved to see her try.

"I don't know, Mom. Jackson is the real challenge. Maybe we should team up," Penny said, winking at Jackson.

Again he was hit with the lack of good memories like this from his childhood. His mother barely acknowledged him, let alone sat down to play games. He'd been more worried about keeping his siblings fed and happy at the time, and he felt a deep ache in his chest. What would it have been like to grow up in a family like this?

They played for quite a while, alternating winners between the three of them. Mrs. M. was passing out the cards for the last game, and Jackson leaned back to stretch.

"Jackson, do you like my sister?" Penny said with pursed lips.

Jerking forward, Jackson hit his elbow on the edge of the table, sending a numbing sensation through his arm. After the pain ebbed away, he said, "Yes, I like your sister."

"Do you *like* like her?" He couldn't help but laugh at Penny's mischievous smile.

"Yes." He wasn't sure what else to say. The minute the word escaped his lips, he felt a warmth spread throughout him, confirming what he'd realized the night before.

"But what's going to happen when you go back to Australia? How will you date her then?"

Jackson picked up the cards in front of him, arranging them in the order he liked, and then lifted his eyes to Penny's. "I'm not quite sure. But it's something to talk about."

"That's good. I like you, but I don't think Hailey would move to Australia. She has a hard enough time eating American food, let alone something she's not used to, like vegemite."

A chuckle escaped his lips, and he shook his head. "You never know. People can surprise you."

"They definitely can," Mrs. M. piped in.

Jackson's mind spun with the information, and Penny's question had thrown him off guard. He'd thought about pursuing a relationship with Hailey, but he hadn't nailed down all the facts about the long-distance thing. And if they were to get married, would he have to relocate everything to California?

He blew out a breath at the thought of marriage. It was something he hadn't given much thought to until he'd come here. His company had survived this long without him fully involved, only checking in from time to time. Maybe he could make it all work. But he'd need more time with Hailey before he started shopping for engagement rings.

He tucked the thought into the back of his mind, making a note to ask Hailey what she thought of their relationship and possible future. He was so focused on it that he messed up, losing the game to Penny. And for once, the competitive streak in him didn't mind.

CHAPTER 25

*P*ulling into her mother's driveway, Hailey paused a moment before getting out of the car. The past few days had been both wonderful and scary, making her wonder if things really could work out between her and Jackson. Australia and California weren't next door to one another and several hours of flying meant they wouldn't get as much time together when they actually visited. But her father had always said to follow her heart, and so far it hadn't led her astray. Maybe it was something she just needed to give a chance.

When Hailey arrived at her mom's house, she walked toward the kitchen, hearing voices floating down the hall. They must not have heard the door open as they talked and played cards.

When Penny asked Jackson about his feelings for her sister, Hailey held her breath, wondering what he would say. The fact that he *like* liked her made her grin so wide it hurt her cheeks. But the next question about dating when he went back to Australia had thrown her for a loop, bringing up the fears she'd just been thinking about.

The other worry she had was that they were from two different sides of the world and from completely different social classes. While Hailey earned good money being a real estate agent, she could never compare to the billions that made up Jackson's fortune. But did he care? He acted as though the gap didn't matter.

The question was, was she okay with it? She'd seen Avery throw money at everyone to get what he wanted, and the minute he was in trouble, he'd reacted in the worst way. But her mother's words echoed in her mind. The only things Avery and Jackson had in common were that they played sports at one time and had money.

Penny's comment about her not wanting to live outside of California stung, and Hailey walked away, standing next to the front door for a few minutes. Calming down enough, she opened the door and shut it a little more forcefully this time.

The movement brought her mother's voice sailing from the kitchen. "Hailey? Is that you?"

After walking down the short hallway, Hailey came around the wall and smiled at them as she put her purse on the island.

"Yep, it's me. Who's winning over here?" She tried to keep her voice light as she put a hand on the back of Penny's chair, but it seemed the emotions churning inside her turned the tone flat.

Penny looked up and grinned at her. "Well, it started out as a pretty good competition, but it seems like Jackson has his mind in the stars right now. Can we go get something to eat for dinner?" Her little sister looked around at the table, and their mom nodded.

"That sounds like a great idea. Since you decided not to cook tonight, I'm not really in the mood to." Her mother's voice sounded weary, and from the puffiness under her eyes, Hailey wondered how much she'd been sleeping.

The group decided on an Italian restaurant just a few blocks away, and Hailey ended up sitting across the table from Jackson. Seeing the blue eyes stare at her as a smile played on his lips, the giddy feeling resurfaced, especially remembering he'd said he liked her.

Who was this she was becoming and what happened to the sensible Hailey? She was acting like a seventh-grader excited about a crush on a boy. But looking up at Jackson, she felt a tug pulling her closer to him. Pushing aside her mother's warning, she knew she wanted to keep seeing him. They were adults, and they could talk about whatever would come their way.

It would make things interesting once he had to go home in a couple of weeks. Would she be able to fly out to see him often? Or would he even have time to fly back here? It sounded like things were getting really busy in Australia, and he'd only been able to rearrange his schedule because of her father's funeral. Would she be enough of a draw for him to make the time to come back now?

Dinner was relaxing and fun. Hailey was grateful to see her mother having a good day, and she had laughed when they'd brought up a funny story about Hailey's father. Maybe it was because they'd been dragging her out of the house for the past few days, but her color seemed to be returning to normal, even if the bags stayed the same.

Her mom and Penny headed up to bed when they got home, and Hailey put away the games from earlier. Walking back into the room, she checked a text message.

"What are you thinking about right now?" Jackson's deep voice sounded across the few feet between them.

She smiled and said, "That I'm not all that tired yet. I'll probably be cursing myself in the morning for all these late nights, but I enjoy hanging out...with you." Her pulse quickened as she said it, and she wasn't sure what to do with her hands, finally placing them behind her back.

He didn't laugh, and his face turned serious. "I was thinking about sitting on the porch swing. Do you want to come out with me?"

"I'd like that," she said, moving toward the front door and onto the porch. She couldn't stop grinning, and her excitement overrode all of the earlier turmoil of worrying about her future with Jackson.

She turned around and saw that Jackson had disappeared. Bending to look inside, she turned her head back and forth, searching for him, when he appeared again, walking out of the living room with a large blanket.

"I figured we could use this. It gets a bit chilly when the sun goes down."

Hailey nodded and settled next to Jackson on the porch swing her father had hung for an anniversary gift several years ago. Always the quiet romantic, in his own way.

Jackson draped the blanket over both of them, and Hailey moved closer so their arms were touching. She waited to feel the electric charge, and sure enough, her arm was tingling.

"How was work today?" she asked Jackson. He'd mentioned several meetings and stuff he needed to catch up on while they'd been looking at properties the day before. There had been several times she'd wanted to text or call him, but then she'd start to worry about everything all over again and tried to focus on other things. She also didn't want to push him away by making him think she was clingy.

He threw back his head and faked a crying face, causing her to laugh. When he straightened up, he chuckled. "It was good. Something I needed to do, especially since I've been gone for a few days. But I think we have all of the problems resolved for today, so that's a good thing."

Hailey bit the bottom of her lip, trying to decide if she wanted to ask the questions plaguing her. "Do you get away a lot? Or do you have to stick around Australia for the most part?"

He looked at her for a moment and then turned his head to look out over the rest of the front porch. "Well, I used to think I was too busy and couldn't get away. But coming here made me realize it's possible to work remotely from time to time. I have a lot of great people working for me, and we're still in the process of researching a new headset, so that makes things a little easier too. When we have a new prototype coming out, I like to be there to make sure everything works correctly."

Hailey was impressed by that. He wasn't someone who was just trying to make a quick buck, but he was invested in the products he created.

They swung back and forth a bit, glancing out at the sprinkling of stars in the sky. His voice seemed to echo in her chest when he asked, "What about you? Do you get out a lot, or does work consume you?"

She felt as if a rock was pinned against her chest took slow, shallow breaths. She'd never thought about it that way, but she worked so much that her free time was very limited and usually involved heading to her parents' home. She hadn't been out with friends in months, and her last date had been nearly a year ago.

"I guess you could say I'm a workaholic. I think it was so I could succeed, so I could show everyone I wasn't a failure and could be something."

"What made you think you'd be a failure?" His gaze made her feel paralyzed, and she just wanted to stare into his eyes a while longer.

Finally, she looked away from him, not sure if she was ready to divulge her little secrets. When she turned back, he was still staring at her, his eyes soft and pulling her in. She could trust him, and that was something she hadn't felt in some years.

"I already kind of told you about it. My dad being disappointed when I didn't want to do social work anymore, that I was quitting too easily. But I also had a boyfriend around the end of college and two years or so after that. He was from a rich family; 'old money,' he used to call them. At first he made me feel like I was amazing and that I could do everything I'd ever dreamed of. But after the first six months, it was like I wasn't meeting his specific rules or the perfect-girlfriend status.

"I kept trying, wanting to please him because I thought I loved him. I see it now, but the way he treated me was not how a boyfriend should treat his girl. The last straw came when I found out about his gambling debts. I'd wondered if he was cheating on me for several months before but could never find any proof."

Jackson's hand moved under the blanket and interlaced his fingers with hers, squeezing to give her reassurance. The warmth of his hand calmed the emotions the memories dredged up.

"One night, we were eating takeout at my apartment when he got a call from his bookie. The man was calling in his debts, and if Avery didn't have the money by the next morning, he would make sure he paid it back. We argued, and he asked to borrow money from me, close to fifty thousand. I didn't have even ten thousand to give him, and he flew off the handle, calling me several names that still make me shudder. And then he hit me." She paused, taking in a sharp breath as the memory took her right back, feeling the pain of his fist against her face.

Jackson tensed next to her and then pulled her closer to him, her head on his shoulder. "I'm so sorry. I watched my mother get beat by one of her boyfriends. It's scary for everyone. Were you okay?"

"I ended up with a concussion and several stitches above my eye. I got in a few good swipes and broke his nose. After a call to the cops, they took him to jail for the night. His parents bailed him out, saying it was all my fault that he'd reacted that way. He lost one of his bigger endorsements because of the whole thing, and then the doctors couldn't set his nose completely straight." She smiled, relishing in that triumphant memory.

Jackson turned, locking eyes with her. "So, did you see him again after that?"

Hailey saw the moment of worry in his eyes, and she laid her head back against his chest, hearing his heart beat at a steady rhythm. "A month later, he kept calling and bugging me, wanting to get back together. He even went so far as to call my parents, trying to get them to persuade me to take him back. The whole situation was hardest for my mother. She'd loved Avery and thought he was the perfect guy for me. But it was pretty hard to dispute the physical evidence." A tear ran down her cheek, and she wondered what had made her talk about all this after so long.

"He was an athlete?"

Hailey nodded. "Baseball player for the Angels. He got injured a few years ago, getting moved down to triple-A." She paused a moment. "A friend told me in passing. I don't keep tabs on him or anything."

Jackson's face brightened, as if he'd just had an epiphany about something. "So that's why you don't like football or athletes or people with money." It was more fact than a question.

She looked down at the colorful shapes of the quilt and whispered, "I guess I just lumped together everyone who reminded me of him at all, assuming they would end up treating me the same way."

"I'm so sorry, Hailey. Is that why you were so suspicious when you found out I made some good investments in my life? You wondered if it had been through gambling?" He smiled at her, and she snorted, reaching her hand up to cover her mouth and nose.

When the laugh subsided, she said, "That was part of it. I think it was more the combination of being a football player and remembering the parents who would try to manipulate my dad into letting their kids play more. Avery fits into the category of throwing money around whenever it suits him. It just rubs me the wrong way, you know? It gave me a bad taste toward wealthy people."

Jackson nodded, and she said, "What about you? Any crazy ex-girlfriends in your closet?"

"I wish I could say no. I dated a girl from my sophomore year of college to March of my senior year. She found out I wasn't getting drafted into the NFL and told me she'd moved on. That I had started with nothing and without a pro contract, I would turn out to be nothing. She went after one of my teammates who got drafted to one of the California teams." He paused, a smile playing on his lips. "It made me feel better that she broke up with him after a career-ending injury."

"Wow! She dumped you because you weren't going to the NFL? Did you even want to play professionally?" Hailey studied his face and watched as his jaw worked back and forth.

Jackson shook his head. "I like football, but I wanted to do something else with my life. Not that being a punter is the most dangerous job in football, but any little injury could be the end of your career, and I didn't want to worry about that at the start of every game."

"Did you play rugby in Australia?"

"As much as a kid with no money can. I was never on an organized club team, but I played as often as I could at breaks or with some kids in the neighborhood. I think it was just sports in general that I loved. Starting the sporting goods store was so kids had the opportunity to learn about other sports."

Hailey moved her arm out from under the blanket to tuck a piece of hair behind her ear. Darn flyaways. She had a thought and asked, "What does the CC stand for in your company?"

Jackson grinned. "It means Coffin Corner. It's a little section of field right next to the end zone and the out-of-bounds line. I was really good at kicking it there, meaning it was as far away as possible for the other team to get to the end zone. It was a little nickname the guys gave me while I was playing."

She'd heard her father talking about coffin corner a couple of times but hadn't realized that it was probably connected to Jackson, just like most of his other stories.

She laid her head on his shoulder, and they swung back and forth in silence. Hailey didn't mind. This was the most relaxed she'd been in years, and she wasn't ready to give that up just yet.

CHAPTER 26

Going through his emails the next morning, Jackson saw one with a headline reading, "Benefit for Mission: Adopted," and he clicked it. Mission: Adopted was the first charity he'd begun to support when money started to come in, wanting to do something to help kids avoid going through the same situation he had. They were based out of LA but the email looked to be forwarded by his secretary, and seeing the original send date was from two weeks ago, he wondered what had happened.

Mr. Walker,

I apologize that this is getting to you so late. I found it in one of my other folders when I was cleaning it out today. I know you don't like to attend these events very often, but I thought, considering the charity, you might be interested.

I hope all finds you well in California.

His secretary's signature ended the note, and Jackson looked below it, reading the original email.

As he read through the few paragraphs, the last line invited him to come to a benefit being held the following Saturday:

As one of our greatest supporters, we wanted to thank you for all you've contributed to our program. Please join us on Saturday, January 25, in cele-brating the adoption of five thousand children last year.

So much for being anonymous.

Five thousand kids adopted into a real home. It was something he'd wanted for as long as he was in foster care, and that overrode the irritation that people had been able to contact him.

A benefit in LA this Saturday night. It was almost too good to be true. It had been a while since he'd been to one of these things, as he usually sent one of his employees to have a night out. But as he thought about the stuffiness of those kinds of events, he pictured Hailey at his side, dressed up for the occasion. Something about that thought calmed him, and he smiled.

The one thing that made him hesitate about dialing her right then was her comment the night before about rich people trying to throw their money about. That was ninety percent of the people who attended these functions. But if she was with him, would she feel the same?

She came to pick him up just after breakfast to go hunting for property once more. As he got in the car, he smiled at her, remem-bering the simple night they'd enjoyed on the swing. He had wanted to kiss her again, but the opportunity never presented itself. But just sitting by her, holding her hand, had been plenty of fireworks anyway.

"I've got some new properties we can look at. Hopefully, we find 'the one' soon so you can get things rolling." She put the car in reverse and pulled out of the driveway.

"Awesome. I hope we find something too. I, uh, I've got something to ask you." Jackson looked at his fingers, willing her to say yes before he'd even asked her the question. "So, there's this benefit I've been invited to, and it's one of my favorite charities. I want to know...will you, uh, will you come with me?" He finally raised his eyes to look at her.

She'd stopped at a stop sign, so she turned to look at him.

"You want me to go to fancy dinner? Are you sure you're feeling okay?" She winked at him, and Jackson laughed. In a softer tone, looking forward as she continued to drive, she said, "I'd love to go with you. When is it?"

"This Saturday. It's formal dress, so if you want, you can use my card to get something." Jackson scrunched his face, knowing how awkward that sounded. She was a hardworking woman, and that was probably the worst suggestion he'd ever made.

He loved the light, airy sound coming from her as she laughed, easing the awkwardness a notch. "I can take care of it. But I always like an excuse to go shopping. Do you have a tux?"

"I'll get on it when we're done today. Maybe you should take your mom and Penny. I'm sure they'd love to help you out with their opinions," Jackson laughed, and she started to as well.

She nodded. "Yeah, Penny would love to give her opinion about anything. Besides, I think there's a dance coming up at her school soon. She might just steal all my thunder." She smiled at him before pulling out onto the road.

Reaching over, he placed his hand over hers and said, "I don't think that's possible."

Her cheeks colored, and she rolled her eyes at him before grinning. He was going to have the most beautiful date at the benefit.

CHAPTER 27

Standing in the dressing room of the local formal dress shop, Hailey worried that she'd never find something by Saturday. The shop wouldn't have anything tailored by that time, and the rest of the dresses seemed to be made for girls that wore size 0 and had no curves whatsoever.

Walking out of the dressing room in the fifth dress, she looked at her mom, who shook her head. "It's just not right, Hailey, dear. Do they have something in green or a pink?"

Scowling, Hailey said, "You know I don't like pink, Mom."

"Yes, but it looks amazing on you. Why don't we at least try one on and see?"

Flopping into the chair next to her mother, Hailey leaned her head back. "It's no use, Mom. I'll just have to tell Jackson I couldn't find a dress on such short notice."

"You will not tell him that," her mother said, her tone firm. "Let's go look more."

Penny had already tried on at least six dresses she was in love with, and Hailey felt a pang of jealousy. If only it were that easy to find a dress she loved.

After fifteen minutes and a lap around the entire store, Hailey wondered if she'd ever be able to look at dresses again. Her mother's arm looked as if it was going to fall off with the number of them draped across it. Squished in the middle of bright pinks and greens was a light blue dress that Hailey hoped would fit. Then she wouldn't have to touch the pink ones.

But in the dressing room, to her dismay, the blue one hugged too much around her hips, making it difficult to pull up to her shoulders. The two green dresses Hailey had approved of on the rack didn't quite work either. As if she weren't already worried, there were only three dresses left hanging on the hook, and she wasn't that thrilled about any of them.

Her mother's face about the first two pinks was lackluster, and Hailey resigned herself to having to wear a plastic bag to the gala. Pulling on the last dress, she was surprised to find that it slid over her curves and around her shoulders with ease. She zipped the back as much as she could and took a look in the mirror.

The faint pink tulle flared out at the bottom, brushing the floor. The top sported beads a shade darker than the tulle, sewn into small flowers. The thick straps covered her shoulders and made her feel at ease. Even in pink.

Walking out, the look on her mother's face was priceless. "Oh, honey. This looks amazing." She twisted her lips as she looked at her daughter and asked, "What do you think?"

"I think I'll have to eat my words about pink." She grinned at her mom. "I really like it."

Penny came out of the dressing room in her regular clothes, and her hands flew to her mouth. "You look so good. Jackson is going to die when he sees you in that."

Her mother stood up and came over, wrapping Hailey in a bear hug. "You look beautiful, darling. He's going to love the dress." Pulling back, she had tears in her eyes, and Hailey had to look away before she started crying too.

"Mom, don't cry. It's not like this is my wedding dress or anything."

"I know," her mom said, sobbing. "I just, I feel bad about what I said the other day. Just know that I love you and I just want the best for you. If the best is Jackson, then I couldn't be happier. If it doesn't work out, I know you will make that decision for a good reason."

Hailey laughed as the tears streamed down her face. "Thanks, Mom. That means a lot."

After she changed out of the dress, they walked up to the register, and her mom pulled out her wallet.

"Mom, I've got it."

"No, you don't. I want to get this for you. We haven't been shopping in ages, and I've missed it."

Hailey took her mother's hand and said, "I'm sorry, Mom. Let's do this more often."

A strange thought entered her mind…what if the next time would be for her wedding dress?

CHAPTER 28

*H*ailey hadn't felt this nervous getting ready for anything, even prom. With her hair curled and her makeup done, she slipped into her dress right as the clock said 5:30. Jackson had gone out to run some errands, or so he said, and told her to be ready by then.

She'd wanted to have her mom and Penny help her get ready for the benefit, and she was grateful she had. It would've been hard to get ready by herself, and it was more fun this way. They'd put some music on and sang and danced as they worked, making this a memory Hailey would never forget.

The door downstairs opened and shut, sending Hailey's nerves into overdrive.

"I'll go tell him you'll be ready in a few minutes," her mom said.

She was surprised because this was the most on time she'd ever been while getting ready for a big date. Was this a date? Or did he think of them as just friends and he'd invited her because he didn't know anyone else here? Her stomach twisted, and she pushed back the hope that something more was growing between them.

Penny held up two necklaces, and they both agreed that the second one looked better with the dress. It was a simple string of pearls with matching pearl earrings that her father had given her for graduation from college. It felt appropriate that she would wear something from him tonight.

"Are you ready for this?" Penny asked, practically bouncing up and down.

"As ready as I think I'll ever be. Why am I so nervous?"

"Maybe because this is the first real date you've had since Avery. And I think you kind of like Jackson, maybe even love him." Leave it to Penny to put Hailey in her place. Her sister smiled and hugged her before turning and leaving the room.

Checking her makeup one more time and twisting one of her curls, she smiled at herself in the mirror, hoping to calm the nerves just a bit. Once she moved out of the bathroom, she started down the stairs, the tulle of the dress swishing along with her.

She made it to about the third stair from the bottom, when Jackson moved into sight from the hall.

His jaw dropped, and a wide grin spread across his face. "You look absolutely amazing. Are you ready to go?" He looked at her with those clear-blue eyes, and she had to hold on to the newel post before she tumbled to the ground. That would have been embarrassing.

"Yes, let me just grab my clutch." She felt odd saying such a thing as she usually only had one purse that should be retired by now. But her mother had found a clutch while at another store the day before and bought it for her. Now Hailey just hoped she wouldn't lose it.

She grabbed a shawl and the clutch, pulling the shawl over her shoulders as she moved back to where Jackson stood. She hadn't admired him in a tux until that moment, but, wow, the guy looked amazing. It looked as if it had been made specifically for him, and she could've put her stamp of approval on it. He had a little stubble that he hadn't shaved, and she liked it, drawing her eyes to his strong jaw. What would it be like to kiss him with facial hair?

Shaking her head, Hailey focused on threading one arm through his as he escorted her out the door. She waved to her mom and sister before stepping off the porch, blowing a kiss at each of them for helping her tonight.

Parked in front of the mailbox was a dark limousine, causing her jaw to drop. The last time she'd been in a limo had been a week ago, but it had been for her father's funeral, not a date.

Hailey turned to him and asked, "Did you get this on purpose? Or do they send this for all the attendees of the benefit?"

Jackson chuckled and said, "I figured with us getting dressed up, it might be nice to have a little room. I didn't want you to squash your dress." He opened the door and helped her in and then slid in after her.

She was startled to find another couple sitting on one side. Hailey turned to Jackson and gave him a glare while trying to smile at the same time, trying to figure out who they were. The guy looked somewhat familiar, but things were a little blurry from the past couple of weeks after talking to so many people. It was difficult to place him.

"Hailey, do you remember Tristan? He was at the funeral with me. We've been best friends since Delta Phi, and when I heard he was invited to the same benefit, I asked him to join us with his date." Jackson smiled, and Hailey pasted on a fake smile, trying to be polite.

She wished he'd have told her they would have company with them. Did this mean she was in the friend zone? Because taking this much time to dress up when you aren't forced to go to a dance with some kid in high school did not signify friend, at least in her mind anyway.

"It's nice to see you again, Tristan. Who's your date?" She turned to look at the girl sitting beside Tristan.

The woman straightened her shoulders, and her smile was so ridiculous that Hailey almost couldn't hold back a smirk. "I'm Susie Carmichael. I met Tristan a while ago, but this is the first date we've been on. I'd say this is a smashing first date, don't you agree, Tristan?"

The look on the man's face said he was less than comfortable, but Hailey could imagine what it was like to be invited to benefits and have to find someone to go with every time when you were single.

Could she consider Jackson and herself a couple? At the moment, she would say no. They hadn't talked about anything that serious just yet, and he hadn't bothered to tell her about Tristan and Susie joining them. Relationships lasted on communication, and if he was going to be hiding things from her like Avery had, maybe it would be better to take a step back.

The two couples made small talk as they drove into the city, and Hailey found it odd that Jackson sat with his arm around her but seemed stiff, like he was afraid to be himself all of a sudden. Had she done something wrong in the last five minutes? Or was it because Tristan was in the car?

Brushing it off, she was determined to make this an evening to remember. Jackson would go home sooner or later, and although she didn't know the future, which scared her, she knew she just had to have a little fun and see where things went.

CHAPTER 29

They arrived at a building with large columns out front and several stairs leading up to the main door. Wearing heels was a good idea as it made it necessary to lean on Jackson. At least he was helping her, and the crisp scent of his cologne helped to ease her irritation a bit.

As they walked into the event room, she was blown away by the scope of the decorations and the beauty of it all. Jackson slipped his hand into hers, and it seemed to ground her, helping calm the nerves and doubts that had been building since the limo ride.

She leaned into him and whispered, "Are you okay?"

His jaw worked back and forth, and his posture was stiff. When he finally turned toward her, he gave her a small smile. "I'll be fine. I just get butterflies every time I have to go to something like this. I feel like an imposter sometimes, like I'm just the kid with nothing, dressed up in a nice suit."

Hailey turned so she was facing him and put her hands on his arms. "Remember how amazing you are. You've conquered so much and haven't let the ups and downs in your life change you. I'm here for you tonight if you need to leave early or if you just need to talk. Just let me know." She smiled, staring at him until he looked at her and nodded.

They walked through the room, and Jackson greeted several people, some of whom looked familiar to Hailey. They found their seats, and she was grateful to see Tristan and Susie sitting at their table. At least she could talk to them when Jackson was talking business to some of the men and women milling about.

Dinner was a fancy affair, with several courses and all the food laid out just so. Hailey had attended nice dinners put on by her company, usually for Christmas, but this put those to shame. She wondered what it cost per person to put this event on.

A raffle followed dinner, and the director announced dancing. Once the music started, Hailey just hoped that she didn't make a fool out of herself. Several couples were already on the floor, moving gracefully to the music, and she hoped Jackson had some skills in this area. Or would they just sit there all night?

Tristan reached his hand out for Susie, a solemn expression on his face, and they moved onto the floor.

Hailey tried not to make it obvious that she wanted to dance, but finally Jackson turned to her. "I'm not the best dancer, but would you join me?"

She smiled at him and took his hand, the sparks between them only adding to her excitement. The whole environment made her feel as if she were in some romantic movie, dancing the night away with her love interest.

They stood at the edge of the dance floor, and he placed one hand on the small of her back, the other held out for her hand.

As they moved, Hailey was sure she was falling head over heels in love with him. His steps were so smooth, and it was as though he could sense when she was about to make a wrong step, correcting before anything could happen. All thoughts of being okay with a friendship between them were gone, and she hoped he felt similar.

"Where did you learn to dance like this?"

Jackson grinned, and she was grateful he was holding on to her so she didn't fall to the ground as she swooned. "The guys and I decided to take a ballroom dance class our senior year. I'm sure the teacher wanted to kick us out on several occasions, but we went from awful to mediocre, enough to get us a B."

There was so much about this guy she found amazing, but a voice inside popped up, making her wonder if she deserved him. It was her mother's comment from a few days ago when she'd said, *What are you doing to be on a guy's list?*

So far, very little. But she did her best to push the thought aside, hoping to move past it and keep this night enjoyable for as long as it lasted.

They danced for two songs, the second one much slower than the first, and Hailey couldn't get enough of the cologne Jackson was wearing. As she rested her chin on his shoulder, she wondered if she was really living a fairy tale or if she'd wake up tomorrow with a pretty dress and the clear sight of how her real life was so boring.

Jackson led her back to the table and said, "I've got to use the loo real quick. I'll be back." He winked at her, his features looking much more relaxed now than they had the entire evening.

Hailey felt a rush of heat move to her cheeks. So many conflicting emotions, but the one that stood out most was that she was in love with him.

She took a bite of the dessert in front of her, cheesecake with strawberry sauce poured over it. As she savored the flavors, Tristan sat in his seat again.

"Where's Susie?" Hailey asked, putting down her fork.

"She had to powder her nose or something like that." Tristan sounded bored.

"You don't look thrilled to have her here." She tried to hide a smile by biting her bottom lip.

Tristan almost laughed, the sound turning into more of a cough. His French accent was more noticeable when he said, "No, everyone I asked already had plans for tonight. And it's rough enough to show up alone, believe me. I've done that too many times to count." Tristan took a drink of water and draped his arm across the chair next to him. "So, what's the story with you and Jackson?"

Nothing like straight to the point.

Hailey's mind searched for words, but she still wasn't sure where she stood with him. "We've just been hanging out a little. I'm his real estate agent."

"And the daughter of his favorite coach," Tristan said, cutting her off. "You've got to be more than just a property seller to make him want to come to something like this."

"He asked me. I didn't persuade him to come tonight." She narrowed her eyes as she looked at him. Tall with dark hair and a slight beard, he was attractive but more irritating than anything. Leaning her chin on the palm of her hand, she asked, "Is this one of your charities too?"

Tristan nodded. "Jackson has always been really passionate about it, and seeing how he's my best friend, I wanted to support something that could have changed his life when he was younger." His face had softened, like his defenses had been taken down a bit.

Hailey smiled and nodded, starting to change her view of him when the next words out of his mouth made her want to scream at his questions.

"So, when he goes back to Australia, where does that leave the two of you?" His intense stare caused Hailey to look down at her hands.

With resolve, she raised her gaze back to his. "Honestly, I'm not sure yet, but that's okay. We've known each other for less than two weeks, and it would be an adventure to keep dating long distance, but I'm willing to do that."

Tristan folded his arms and pierced her with a sad look. "Has he told you about Katie O'Brien?" The name didn't ring a bell, but then again, Jackson hadn't told her his ex's name.

"Is that his ex-girlfriend?" Hailey asked.

He nodded. "Did he tell you what he went through when she dumped him?"

"The summary," she said, trying to tamp down the panic threatening to take over. Did she even know Jackson? The trust she'd felt building between them was like a pencil that had pressure applied to both sides, threatening to snap.

"I'm not trying to make you nervous or anything," Tristan said, waving his hand in the air. "I just want you to know that, as his best friend, I do my best to keep people from hurting him. Jackson is a nice guy, the best, actually. That's both a blessing and a curse for him."

Hailey held up her hands. "Believe me, the last thing I want to do is hurt him. I really like him and hope there is something more between us. That maybe we just haven't talked about it."

"Or maybe he's just too scared you're going to break his heart like she did."

How was Jackson friends with this guy? Maybe he needed someone who was harsh and to-the-point to keep him grounded. It was the only thing she could think of to connect the two opposite personalities.

"He acted as though it hadn't hurt him much." She raised her eyebrow as if to challenge him.

Tristan expression was vacant, as if he'd had to describe all this several times before. "I was there for the whole thing. The only reason Jackson graduated was because I dragged him to class and made sure he turned in his assignments. In between those times, he didn't leave his bed, preferring to get lost in a world of video games and an enormous amount of chips."

Trying to picture that side of Jackson, she realized it could be possible. He was such a sweet guy that having a girl tell him she no longer loved him probably came as a shock.

"This Katie was really that bad?"

"She's just a gold digger, and when she saw that Jackson had no desire to go to the NFL, she latched on to the next best thing. It took a while for Jackson to realize that she'd broken up with him, as she just stopped responding to calls and texts. It was only after several eyewitness accounts of her with the other teammate that it hit him hard."

Hailey couldn't keep her mind from darting in twenty different directions, all trying to make sense of what this would mean for her own relationship with Jackson.

Before she had the chance to say anything else, Tristan raised his hand and pointed behind her, a look of shock changing his nonchalant features.

Hailey turned, not sure what he was pointing at. Scanning the room, she spotted Jackson on the dance floor, looking surprised as a brunette with hair cascading to the middle of her back stood in front of him, just inches away. Her moves were exaggerated as she spoke.

Hailey turned back to Tristan. "Who is that?"

Tristan looked as though he'd been slapped as the color drained from his face. "Katie O'Brien."

"What?" Hailey whipped her head around to Jackson, feeling her heartbeat in her throat. They were too far away to read how Jackson was feeling, and she hesitated, unsure whether she should go out on the dance floor or stay where she was.

"I'm as baffled as you are. We haven't seen her since graduation." Tristan's voice conveyed the shock he was feeling.

Hailey's breath came in short bursts, as if something were squeezing her lungs too hard.

The dancers around them transitioned as the song ended and the next song started out slow. As the couples came together, so did Jackson and Katie. Hailey wasn't sure if Jackson stepped closer to the girl or if Katie closed the space between them, but either idea caused her blood to boil. She felt something pull in her chest, as if her heart were physically tearing itself apart. Like a knife was slicing it in two.

Hailey quickly stood and moved around the dance floor, making her way through the crowd along the sides to get to Jackson. She'd finally moved around two gossiping older ladies, when she looked up to locate Jackson and gasped.

Katie's arms were wrapped around Jackson's neck, her lips pressed to his.

Hailey took a step back, feeling the physical blow. A hammer tapped on the top of the knife already in her chest, pounding it deeper and cutting more with every movement.

Twirling around, Hailey stalked back to the table, grabbing her clutch and fighting the tears that threatened to spill. She wouldn't cry here, where the world could see her pain. Raising her chin, she strode off, her eyes focused on the door.

She hadn't realized Tristan had followed her until she heard his voice from over her shoulder.

"Hailey, don't leave. I didn't know any of that was going to happen. I'm sure he'll be able to tell you what happened and why. He really does like you. I'm sure the kiss was all Katie."

Whirling around, she narrowed her eyes at him. "You've just pestered me for the past ten minutes about how I shouldn't hurt him and that our relationship would never work out. Now you want to say he likes me after he kissed that-that—ugh!" Her brain couldn't pull up a word to describe Jackson's ex, and she groaned before turning back to the door.

As she walked out, she kicked herself for even believing she was ready for love again, especially with Jackson Walker, billionaire. She should have stuck with what she knew to be true about wealthy people. How could she trust a billionaire to be faithful to her when he could have any woman he wanted? When women would be throwing themselves at him everywhere he went?

"It's fine, Tristan," she called over her shoulder. "I'm tired. Just tell him I found my way home." Running out of the large hall, she moved down the steps and out to the busy street. She'd just call a cab rather than spend another moment stuck in an enclosed space with the man she'd thought she could have a future with. The traitor.

She walked down the block a bit, hoping that if Jackson did come looking for her, he wouldn't find her just yet. Her heart was breaking, and there was no way she could handle him saying that he was still in love with his college sweetheart. Part of her knew it probably wasn't true, but she was in no condition to talk about how she felt with anyone.

This was not a Cinderella moment, nor did she want it to be. She just needed some time to wallow, to remember that guys would always break her heart if given the chance. Her trust had broken and she wasn't sure it could ever be repaired.

By the time the cab pulled up alongside her, she was sobbing so much that it was difficult to give directions to her apartment. The cab driver looked at her with pity, but she just wanted to crawl in a hole and sleep for days.

They pulled up to her apartment building twenty minutes later, making her grateful for light traffic for once in her life. As she went to pay the man, he waved her off. "Looks like you could use some good fortune. No charge."

She thanked him and moved inside, feeling the chill of her silent apartment.

Walking into her bedroom she sat on her bed, a fresh wave of emotions washing over her. She lay down, telling herself she needed to change into her pajamas, but she drifted off to sleep instead.

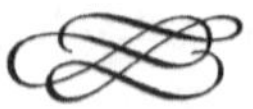

CHAPTER 30

Jackson was walking across the dance floor, returning from the bathroom, when he heard a familiar voice.

"Why, don't you look dashing," Katie O'Brien said with a coy smile.

"What are you doing here, Katie?" he asked.

"I'm here for a benefit, obviously. Although, it was quite a surprise to see you here. How have you been? Did you move back here from Australia?" She widened her eyes and tried to give him the innocent look she'd probably mastered while they'd been dating.

Jackson looked at the wall, disgust filling him when he thought about how hurt he'd been when she'd dumped him. "I was doing really well until you showed up. What do you want, Katie?"

He wanted to push her away and move on, when she said, "I miss you. I made a mistake, and I wish I could go back and fix it. One dance, for old times' sake?" She stepped closer as the music transitioned to a slow dance.

Raising his eyebrows, he took a step back. Did she really think he'd fall for that? "No, Katie. Not a chance."

He started to move back to Hailey, when Katie leaned forward and kissed him, completely catching him off guard.

Her lips barely touched his before Jackson grabbed her arms and pushed her away quickly. He shook his head. "You had your chance. I'm in love with someone else." He turned away and walked toward the table, the words he'd just said ringing like bells in his head.

He was in love with Hailey Montgomery. The girl who listened, the girl who laughed, and the girl who had shown him real love by comforting him instead of worrying about how she looked to the media. She'd never worried about the number of zeroes in his bank account. He loved her more than he thought possible, even more than the puppy love he'd felt for Katie.

When Jackson walked back to the table and saw Hailey wasn't there, he figured she'd gone to the bathroom. But when Tristan made it back from the other side of the room a few minutes later, he informed Jackson that Hailey had seen the kiss.

Guilt ripped through him. What had he been thinking, allowing Katie even a second of his time, letting her get close enough to steal a kiss?

"Where did she go?" Jackson asked Tristan, his eyes already scanning the crowd.

"She said she'd find her way home. I don't know, man. She looked pretty crushed. I don't think she wants to have anything to do with you right now." Tristan walked next to him as Jackson moved through the crowd. "Are you having second thoughts about Katie?"

Frowning, Jackson looked at his best friend. "Of course not. I love Hailey."

Relief washed over Tristan's face. "Good. Because I don't think I can take heartbreak, round two."

"Shut up and help me find her." Jackson pushed Tristan's shoulder. Time was not on his side if he was going to find Hailey and explain. He didn't dare think about what she was feeling right now.

He walked out the front doors and scanned the crowd as he took the stairs two at a time. Running one way down the street, he turned to run back, but there was no sign of her.

Catching the next cab, he gave the address to the Montgomery home, hoping she'd be there tonight. He'd never been to her apartment and didn't know any real specifics about where it was.

"See ya later, Tristan," he called as he waved at his friend. "The limo's all yours."

"Good luck, man," Tristan called. "You're going to need it!"

What had he done? Would Hailey hear him out? He'd just hurt her like her ex had hurt her, after everything she'd confessed to him about her fears. How was he going to convince her that the kiss she'd seen hadn't been something he'd wanted? Would she be able to trust him again?

The ride seemed to take forever, and he just hoped she'd listen. She could be bullheaded and stubborn, but he usually admired those qualities in her. He just hoped they wouldn't work against him tonight.

* * *

THE FRONT DOOR WAS OPEN, and he was grateful for it. Glancing at the large clock on the entry wall, he noticed it wasn't yet eleven. Running up the stairs, he checked Hailey's bedroom and then ran down the hall and knocked on the master.

Mrs. M. answered the door a few seconds later, her tired eyes shooting open when she saw the look on his face. "Jackson, what's wrong? Where's Hailey?" Her eyes darted up and down his body, probably looking for some sign of injury.

"She left. I was hoping she'd come back here." Panic set in, and he was ready to run to her apartment right then if her mother would give him the address.

Pulling on a robe, she urged him to move downstairs to the living room, pointing for him to sit on the couch. She sat at the other end, leaning forward with worry etched on her face.

"Tell me what happened."

Jackson began, giving an abridged version of the night's events but with enough details to let her know it was all his fault.

"Mrs. M., where is her apartment? I've got to explain to her what happened."

Shaking her head, the woman in front of him gave him a sad smile. "I'm sorry, Jackson. You know how I feel about you, but she's my daughter. You'll need to give her some time. Let her decide how she feels about the situation."

Throwing out his arms to emphasize his plea, he said, "Please, Mrs. M., I love her."

A look of happiness passed over her face before she returned to her sad look. "I messed up when she broke up with Avery. I won't go against her wishes now." She leaned forward and took Jackson's hand, squeezing it. "It will work out how it should. Just know that I'm rooting for you." With a smile, she wrapped him in a hug before leaving the room.

Was there another way to find out where she lived? He trudged up to his bedroom and slumped onto the bed. Why hadn't he run the other way the minute Katie spoke to him? He'd be dancing with the most beautiful girl right now if he had.

Sending up a plea to the heavens, he fell asleep, hoping that the morning would bring the opportunity to explain.

$\mathcal{A}$ knock sounded at the door, and Jackson turned, seeing through the window that the sun's rays were only barely peeking over the horizon. He stood up and walked to the door, hoping it was Hailey. For the second time that week, his disappointment came in the form of Penny.

"You slept in that?" she asked, pointing to his clothes.

Looking down, he saw the wrinkled tux and groaned. The events from last night were no nightmare.

"Yes. It's been a rough night."

Penny leaned in, looking around conspiratorially. "I may have heard your conversation with my mom last night. She might be trying to stick with Hailey's choices, but I don't have to." She reached out her hand, placing a piece of paper in Jackson's palm. "Here's her address. I'd go over now."

Jackson moved to unbutton his shirt, thinking he'd better change before barging into her apartment.

"Leave the tux on. It might help sway your case enough to have her forgive you." Penny smiled at him sadly and then reached forward and wrapped her arms around his middle, giving him a hug.

"Thanks, Penny. I really appreciate this."

He threw on his shoes, ran down the stairs, and pulled the keys from the key ring. Revving the engine a little too hard, he backed out and took off down the street. He felt like he'd been shot out of a gun, going from a dead sleep to an adrenaline-infused hunt for the woman he loved.

Before too long, he pulled up to the address. Parking along the sidewalk, he gripped the steering wheel and took a breath.

"Just tell her the kiss meant nothing and that you love her." It felt like a pep talk her father would have given him years ago.

He ran up the steps and entered the building where he quickly located number eighteen and knocked on the door.

Silence came from the other side of the door, and he checked his watch. It was almost seven in the morning.

He knocked again, the sound echoing in the silent hallway.

Met with the same quiet, he waited some time and raised his hand to knock again, trying to decide if he should just come back later, when the door swung open.

Hailey stood there, and at the sight of her, his heart broke. She was still wearing her dress from the night before, her hair falling out of the pins that had held it in place. The thing that cut him the most was seeing the black trails down her face.

"What do you want?" she said through clenched teeth.

Putting out his hands, worried that she'd slam the door in his face at any moment, Jackson saw he was going to have to explain in a very short amount of time.

"I want you." He made eye contact with her, but instead of the happiness he'd pictured by telling her those words, he saw hardness.

"You have a funny way of showing it."

"Katie kissed me. I pushed away within seconds and came to look for you. You are the one I want, not some girl who changes her mind about what she wants every five months." He rolled his lips in, afraid of what she might say.

It took her a moment, but she lifted her chin and said, "I took this assignment, you as the special client, so I could make broker. Along the way, I fell in love with you, thought you were different than the ghosts of my past. You broke my trust. If you really wanted me, you wouldn't have let her near you. I've been burned before and I'm not going to risk my heart to a billionaire who can get any girl he wants and think it's okay. Fidelity is at the top of my list of traits in my future partner and I won't settle."

Her eyes turned glassy, and a single tear trickled down one cheek. She didn't move to wipe it away, only nodded and shut the door with a soft click.

Jackson leaned against the door. "Please, Hailey, don't do this. I love you, not her. Please, just don't give up on me."

Silence was all he heard on the other side, and a dull ache formed in his chest. How had things gotten so messed up so fast?

Running his hand through his hair, he turned and walked back to the car. Tears came pouring down, and he wished he could go back and redo the entire evening.

CHAPTER 32

Several weeks passed, and March arrived, but Hailey barely noticed. She'd wallowed the day after the benefit, and then she'd gone back to work Monday morning, knowing she had to stick with what she knew best. Her mother told her that Jackson had taken a flight back to Australia that afternoon. Hailey had hoped to be grateful for that, but it just hurt worse, knowing he'd left even with her as mad as she was at him.

The only problem was that six weeks had gone by in a mindless blur, and she'd barely registered them. When she checked the calendar and saw it was the eighth of March, she almost broke down crying, hoping the chasm in her chest would soon be healed. She thought that after so long, she'd be able to breathe normally instead of having to take shallow gasps.

Jackson had called and texted several times, but she didn't want to give herself hope when she knew nothing would change. The messages had stopped four days ago, and she wished she hadn't been counting the time, as if by day seven things would go back to normal and she'd be happy again.

"Jonathan told me to bring these in for you to sign," Cindy said at the door. It was an odd request to ask the receptionist to bring back papers, but Hailey wasn't in the mood to question it.

"What are they?" she asked, trying to make her voice sound more chipper. She'd received more than a few lectures from her mother the past month about how she needed to stop being such a crab.

Cindy looked down at the papers. "It says here these are commission papers for that office space down on Main Street."

Hailey's head popped up. "The old bookstore?"

The older woman nodded and handed Hailey the papers.

Scanning the first few pages, Hailey couldn't find anything that showed who'd signed for the lease. "Do you know who is leasing out the place?"

Cindy leaned in, dropping her voice to a whisper. "It's not a lease. It seems someone bought the whole block of buildings. You get a commission on all of it."

"Who was it, though?" She felt a lump growing in her throat and hoped to keep the tears at bay. After several days of tears right after the benefit, it was as though she'd turned into a desert and hadn't teared up at anything since. Why would she suddenly be able to now?

The papers told her nothing, only showing a DHM in the buyer line. She stood, taking the papers to Jonathan's office. One of the other agents was sitting in the chair opposite him, but she was too focused to notice.

Waving the papers across the desk, she asked, "Who bought the old bookstore?"

Shrugging, Jonathan said, "It was kept anonymous. The realtor lives in London and said his client wanted to buy the entire block. Since you represented the bookstore, you get the commission."

Something about the situation didn't seem right. Who would want to buy the entire block? There was a flower shop on one side of the old bookstore and a popular diner on the other. Would they be kicking out the other businesses?

Anger boiled within her. It was the first spark of feeling she'd had in weeks. She just hoped the buyer didn't decide to knock everything down and build a high-rise. Anaheim Hills wasn't exactly a city, but the older touches down Main Street made her hope it wouldn't change for a long time.

* * *

PULLING up to her mother's house, Hailey checked her appearance in the mirror. She pinched her cheeks to add some color to her pale face and made sure to swipe back the few strands of hair that had escaped her ponytail.

She hadn't made it up the porch steps when Penny came bounding out. "You'll never guess what I heard today."

Not in the mood to play any games, Hailey said, "Just tell me."

Their mother walked out the door and said, "Not yet, Penny. Let's go. We'll take my car, Hailey."

Frowning, Hailey looked between the two of them. "Go where? I just got here, and all I want is food and sleep. The construction in my building started at six thirty again this morning."

"I'm sorry, dear. We're on our way to get food now."

It sounded good enough for Hailey, and she sat in the passenger seat, checking several emails while her mother drove down the road. Soon enough, her mother parked, and Hailey looked up, doing a double take.

"Why are we at the old bookstore?" Her heart sped up as she saw lights on in the building and, glancing through the windows, rows and rows of books. She opened her door and climbed out, peering in through the glass door.

"We can go in, Hailey. But you need to move so I can open the door," Penny said.

Hailey only registered the words after Penny opened it, hitting her on the arm.

Walking inside, Hailey's mouth dropped open as she stared at all the bookshelves stacked with books, with several large shelving units set in the middle of the built-ins along the walls. The back corner had an overstuffed chair with a small table in front of it. This had been her favorite place as a kid, and she wondered if this was real.

Spinning back to look at her mother, she asked, "Someone is reopening the bookstore?"

Her mother smiled and nodded. "It will be open for business in the morning."

"Do you know who it is?"

Penny's phone rang, and their mother turned, curious about the caller. Moving toward the back of the store, Penny's voice grew softer as she moved away, making it harder for Hailey to control what little patience she had.

"Mom, please tell me what's going on. Why are we here, and who is restarting the bookstore?"

"Jackson."

The answer set Hailey back on her heels, blindsided by the revelation. "What do you mean, Jackson? He's back in Australia. Why would he care about this space?"

"Because he loves you. He's been trying to think of a way to show you, and this was his answer."

"Did you tell him to do this?" Hailey felt irritation well up, hoping she wasn't betrayed by her mother after the Avery situation.

Shaking her head, her mother said, "No. I haven't talked to him in a few weeks. He contacted me today and said to bring you over."

Hailey tried to figure out why he would have decided to do this. The only time she'd been here with him was that first day of property hunting, when she'd told him about the outings with her mother.

"What did he name it?" Her throat had gone dry, making her voice sound more scratchy than she was used to.

"Head outside and see."

Without waiting, Hailey took long strides across the room and pushed at the glass door. Turning, she saw two men revealing a covering from the sign. Once the paper was gone, she gasped. "Montgomery's Bookstore" shone back at her in a bright blue.

Her mother exited the bookstore and stood next to her, wrapping an arm around Hailey's waist.

Penny came out and Junior met them from down the block. The two of them looked at Hailey and grinned.

Hailey felt her hands shaking. "You all knew about this?"

"Jackson called today. He hadn't told us anything until about an hour ago. He just said there was a surprise that was finally ready and we should bring you here." Penny grinned, and Hailey wasn't sure how to feel about the whole thing.

"Why would he do this? He's probably just throwing money around. Something Avery would do."

"No, that's not how Jackson works," Junior said, shocking the three women around him. He'd been near silent since Jackson left, only answering questions in grunts or one-word phrases. "His store is going in on the other side of the block, since the paper company went out of business. But He sent you this." He pulled out a small envelope from his pocket and handed it to Hailey.

Her name was scrawled on the envelope in Junior's handwriting. She slid her finger through it, releasing the flap. Pulling the paper out, she unfolded what looked like the printout of an email.

She looked around at her family, unsure she was ready for whatever he had to say. After weeks of the ups and downs of emotions, would all this fix her relationship with Jackson?

My Dearest Hailey,

I know you've probably heard enough from me over the past few weeks. I've been doing everything I can to show you how I truly feel, that you are the one I want to be with.

I could tell from your face that the old bookstore meant a lot to you. It holds the kind of memories I wish I'd had growing up, and I couldn't bear to turn it into anything but what you remembered.

I know what you're probably thinking, that I used my wealth to try and change your mind. Just know that I was planning to do something in your father's memory since I arrived there for the funeral. This seemed like the perfect tribute to him as well as guarding something you loved from your past. I've set it up so that all proceeds will go toward a scholarship for one or two students at Hawthorne each year.

I hope one day you'll forgive me. I love you, Hailey, more than I thought possible.

With much love,

Jackson

TEARS STREAMED down Hailey's face, and she did her best to wipe them away. She should be furious, should get him out of her mind and heart forever for trying to win her affections. But he hadn't sent flowers or jewelry or chocolates. He'd created something to honor her father's memory and a way for students to get an education.

Her mother wrapped her other arm around her, pulling her close.

"He didn't kiss that girl," Penny said, causing Hailey to look up.

Frowning, Hailey asked, "How do you know? You weren't there." All the emotions from the night of the benefit came barreling back, and Hailey felt more pain than she had in weeks.

"Jackson came home and told Mom the whole story that night." Penny's arms were crossed over her chest, and she stared at Hailey with a challenge on her face.

Stepping back from her mother, Hailey looked at her, searching her face for answers. "Is that true, Mom?"

Nodding, her mother said, "He came home, frantic, trying to find you. He told me his ex-girlfriend showed up and kissed him but that he didn't feel anything for her. You should have seen his face, Hailey. He looked like the world was ending, and he told me he loved you."

Penny chimed in and said, "He asked for the address to your apartment, but Mom wouldn't give it to him."

"He still showed up the next morning."

"Because I gave him your address. The guy loves you, Hailey. He's probably the greatest person ever, and the bonus is that he was trained by Dad. You're not going to find someone better for you than him."

"I've been emailing and texting him while he's been gone." Junior's voice again caused the other three to turn with rapt attention. "He always asks how you are, what you've been doing. He misses you."

Hailey wanted to be mad at her family for keeping all of these secrets, but all she could think about was Penny's words. Everything she'd seen from Jackson had been positive, and the fact that he'd learned a lot from her father made him even more attractive to her. Maybe she'd jumped to conclusions and Katie had taken advantage of the situation. Jackson at least deserved the chance to explain it.

Penny stepped forward, touching Hailey's arm, and asked, "Do you love him?"

Nodding, a tear slid down her cheek. "I do. I think I have since our first day looking for properties."

"Then go get him. The next flight to Sydney leaves in about four hours." Penny turned her phone to show several flight options.

Hailey stared at the phone for several seconds before she said, "Let's go. I need to pack."

The four of them jumped into their mother's car and drove through the neighborhoods until they arrived at her apartment. She ran in and threw several shirts, pants, shoes, and a few dresses into the suitcase. Heading back outside, she was grateful to see her family still waiting for her in the car.

"Are you sure about this, honey?" her mother asked, putting the car in drive. "I just want to make sure you're doing this because you want to and not because you feel obligated about the bookstore."

Smiling wide, it was the first real smile she'd shown in weeks. "I love him, Mom."

Her mother reached over and patted her hand. "Then let's get you on that flight."

CHAPTER 33

The fasten-seatbelt sign was lit, and the captain had just announced their final descent into Sydney. After what seemed like the longest trip of her life, she was finally close to Jackson. Every doubt that could have crept into her mind had, from leaving the comfort of California to whether she could survive eating different food. But she kept getting on the connecting flights, doing her best to sleep and keep her mind occupied.

By the time they landed, she grabbed her bag from baggage claim and rented a car. Her phone had just started receiving texts, and she saw one from Junior with Jackson's address and "Good luck!"

Walking out to find the rental car, her phone rang, and she saw it was her boss. She felt a knot in the pit of her stomach as she realized she hadn't even called to tell him she was leaving and wouldn't be in for a while.

"Jonathan, I'm so sorry. I just landed in—"

"Sydney? Yeah, I contacted your mother when you didn't show up yesterday. It seems like that special client turned out to be the one for you, huh?"

"I haven't seen him yet, but I hope so. I'll know more later, but I probably won't be in for a few days."

Jonathan chuckled. "I believe that. Australia is a long flight from here. There is one thing I wanted to talk to you about, and I wanted to do it in person yesterday."

Hailey bit her lip, leaning against the car she'd been assigned.

"The board has decided to make you one of the brokers. At the same time, we want to expand our business to other countries. From all the research we've done, Australia is one of the first places we'd like to set up a branch. Would you want to head that up?"

Excitement burst through her chest and a mixture of anxiety. Move to Australia? Penny's words echoed in her brain that Hailey couldn't live somewhere else. She could handle a lot of things, and moving to another country would be one of them. She'd make sure of it. That is, if Jackson still wanted her.

"I'd love to. But let me get things figured out here before I give the final answer."

"Sounds good. We'll be getting started as soon as possible there, so let me know when you've decided."

Hanging up the phone, Hailey couldn't believe the possibilities. Now she just needed to see where things stood with Jackson.

* * *

JACKSON HAD GOTTEN up early and done some surfing. It was about the only thing that kept him centered the past few weeks. He hadn't heard from Hailey or her family since he'd called about the bookstore being ready, and he was starting to get nervous. Should he just try to forget her? It didn't seem like she would forgive him anytime soon.

Stepping out of the shower, he threw on some shorts and a t-shirt, part of him wishing it wasn't a Saturday morning so he'd have more to do. He didn't require his research team to work on the weekend, and the store didn't need him, as the manager had done a great job while he'd been in California.

Rubbing the towel over his hair, he heard a knock at the door. Not sure who it could be at ten in the morning, he turned the knob, expecting it to be a package he'd ordered a few days before.

Hailey was standing there.

His heart beat faster, and he rubbed at his eyes, just to make sure he wasn't hallucinating about her now.

"Hailey?"

Her lips twisted to the side, and she nodded. He knew what the flights were like from California, but she looked like she'd just left the house to run some errands, her hair pulled high in a ponytail.

"I can't believe it. What are you doing here?"

"Do you mind if I come in?" she asked, pointing inside the door. "I know I've sat in planes for over twenty-four hours, but sleep didn't happen."

"Oh, sorry. I'm just so surprised to see you." Jackson stepped back and waved her in.

She gave him a shy smile and walked past to take a seat on the couch.

Moving to sit next to her, Jackson's mind was filled with questions. He stared at her, still not believing she'd come all this way.

When she spoke, her voice was a whisper. "Thank you for the bookstore. It is something my family will cherish always. And the fact that there will be a scholarship for students, that's a great idea."

With a shrug, Jackson said, "I know how Coach loved Hawthorne, and I figured it would be a good way to honor his memory."

The silence descended again, and Jackson tried to be patient while Hailey sorted through whatever she was going through.

Finally looking him in the eyes, Hailey said, "I've been miserable ever since the benefit. And when my mom told me you'd flown back here, I thought I'd be able to move on. Seeing the bookstore yesterday, or two days ago…" she chuckled and shook her head. "Whenever it was, I realized how much I'd missed you. Having you there to do things with and to listen, it made time without you seem endless and lonely."

Jackson tried to contain his excitement. Everything he'd dreamed over and over again during the past few weeks was happening, right here, in real life.

He took her hands and scooted closer. "Hailey, you have to know that I haven't had feelings for my ex in years. Her kissing me was not something I wanted to happen. I've loved you since I saw you in that bookstore, and I just hadn't realized it until you'd disappeared from the gala. Will you forgive me?"

She glanced down at their hands and then back up at him, nodding. "I love you, Jackson Walker."

Lifting his hands, he cradled her face as he leaned in and touched his lips to hers. Every nerve was on fire. He'd thought he'd never have this chance again, and the experience was even better than their first kiss. Realizing he hadn't responded, he pulled back, grinning at her.

"I love you too." He kissed her again, but it was short as a thought came to his mind. "How are we going to work this? Just fly back and forth to see each other?"

Her face beamed. "Actually, my boss just called when I got off the plane. They are planning on opening a real estate office here in Sydney. So I'm going to be moving here, if that's okay with you."

"Are you kidding me? That's incredible." He leaned forward, kissing her again, this time with more intensity than before. The nerves in his lips felt like a sparkler that filtered throughout the rest of his body. He'd been blessed with a lot of things in his life, but this was the best thing that had ever happened to him. She was here and she wanted to stay. Not like the rest of the people from his childhood.

He pulled back slowly as they caught their breath and whispered, "Then I won't have to dream about the next time I can kiss you."

"Exactly." Hailey said, wrapping her arms around his neck. "I'm yours for as long as you'll have me."

EPILOGUE

*H*ailey had moved to Australia a little more than two months before, and with the help of Jackson, had found a place for the real estate branch, as well as an apartment near his home. There were a few differences living in Australia, but she was surprised to find how much she loved it. Although she didn't think she'd ever develop a taste for vegemite.

One of the best moments of her time there was when Jackson introduced her to his brother and sister, Patrick and Abbey. They'd met at CC Sporting Goods the month before when they were on break from university and since, they'd spent several outings together. Hailey loved seeing the peace in Jackson's face every time, as if part of his dreams of a family had been fulfilled.

Hailey sat on the beach, breathing in deeply after her last run on the water. The two of them had spent the morning surfing, and Hailey found she was slowly starting to get the basics of it. She'd had several reservations when they'd first started, telling him she'd turn into a tomato if left out in the sun for too long. Jackson had just brought her a body suit, which kept her warm as well as guarding her from sunburn.

That morning, she'd been able to catch a few waves and stay up for longer than all the other times combined, and Jackson's face showed his excitement at her progress.

She walked up on the beach, dragging her board behind her. The sun had risen over the horizon, and the bright rays lit up the sky. She could feel the exhaustion in her legs and arms and was grateful for the break after swimming through the waves.

Jackson caught a large wave, zigzagging back and forth along it before it crested and escaping just in time to glide along closer to the beach.

As he walked up to her, he was all smiles, and Hailey couldn't help but smile back. She couldn't imagine continuing life without him at her side, and every day seemed like a gift life had given her.

"You were amazing out there. How did you feel?" he asked.

"Really good. I'll only need ten more years to get to your level." She chuckled, and Jackson threw back his head and laughed.

His face grew serious, and he looked into her eyes, the act still making her stomach turn to goo. "Do you want to go for a walk before we head back? The beach is still somewhat empty."

"Sure."

He reached forward and pulled her up. Interlacing their fingers, he led her down the beach, the sand cool beneath her feet. He didn't say anything, and she wondered what he was thinking about.

When he pulled her to a stop, she looked up and saw a sandcastle that came up to her knee.

"Wow! Someone did a great job with this. My sandcastles always fall down before I can make them this big."

He turned to look at her. "I made it."

She looked up, getting lost in his blue eyes. "You did? When did you have time to do that?"

Jackson gave her a sheepish grin. "I had a hard time sleeping last night."

Hailey raised an eyebrow. "So you came to the beach and made this in the dark?"

The question seemed the relax him, and he chuckled. "Maybe. Look inside."

Hailey took a step forward, peeking over the wall. Inside sat a small red velvet box. She reached in and pulled it out, feeling her pulse speed up.

Jackson knelt in the sand and gently took the box from her.

"I've loved having you here for the past two months. There are so many times when I can't believe I found you, and I want to be with you forever. Hailey Anne Montgomery, will you spend the rest of your life with me?"

She couldn't help the tears streaming down her face as she nodded, reaching out to pull him up. "Yes, yes, I'll marry you."

Pulling him into a hug, she kissed him, grateful for the man who stood before her. Her thoughts turned to her father and she teared up a moment, thinking all of this wouldn't have been the same without him, without that connection between her and Jackson.

"What are you grinning about?" Jackson asked, looking into her eyes.

"I don't know how many times my father talked about you, painting you as the perfect man. It made me wonder if somehow he knew we would end up together. I should have trusted him more, but I guess it's one of those things you learn by experience."

Jackson's eyes moved to the sky and then back to her, that lazy half-smile on his face again. "He's been right about everything else. I wouldn't be surprised if that was his intention all along."

Hailey twisted in Jackson's arms, watching the sun make its full appearance over the horizon.

Coach Montgomery's golden boy and princess were together at last.

* * *

Keep reading for a sneak peak of Roman & Isabelle's story in *The French Billionaire*

* * *

Thank you for reading *Love, Austen!* If you enjoyed it, I would love to see a review from you. You can also subscribe to Britney's newsletter here:

Subscribe to Britney's List

CHAPTER 1

THE FRENCH BILLIONAIRE

Checking her calendar for the day, Juliette Rousseau was grateful for the lighter load. With a meeting scheduled this morning and another for the afternoon, she could finally get out and check several items off her list.

As the owner of Rousseau Belle, a skin care company based in Paris, France, she was constantly in search of new materials to work into her creams and lotions. She employed several people in research as well as production, but having the freedom to pick materials up herself was a rarity these days.

Her assistant, Rachelle, walked into her office with a slight grin on her face. "Your meeting is here a bit early. Do you want me to show her in?"

"Sure, then I can get to the market sooner."

"Okay, I'll let her know." Rachelle walked out of the room and back down the hallway, leaving Juliette in silence once again.

Clicking on the event in her online calendar, Juliette tried to refresh her memory of what it was about. Delacroix Marketing. Ugh.

Just another sales pitch she'd have to turn down, and not just once, but several times as they tried to sweeten the deal to get her business. She was still amazed that she'd been able to create this company after starting from mixing the creams in her parents' home in Dinan. The fact that she now had companies vying for her business was mind-boggling.

Nearly a minute later, a woman walked in, her hand outstretched even before she'd made it all the way through the door.

"Good morning, Madame Rousseau. Thank you for meeting with me. I'm Rose Boucher." She leaned over the desk, and Juliette stood, shaking her hand.

"It's nice to meet you, Madame Boucher. Please have a seat there." Juliette pointed to the chair in front of her desk and then took her own seat, scooting in and waiting for the pitch.

The woman smiled at her, a few age lines around her eyes. The Rousseau Belle aloe cream would be best to combat that. Juliette shook her head, trying to focus on what the woman was saying. Occupational hazard.

"As I told your assistant, I represent the Delacroix Marketing Agency, and we are interested in working with you on your marketing campaigns. It's been proven that advertising with our company and in the right areas can increase revenue by over forty percent."

Juliette raised an eyebrow. "Forty percent? What clients do you currently have?"

Rose rattled off several names, and Juliette nodded.

"So, when you're advertising to men, with sports, beer, and apparel, your companies have seen that significant of an increase. What experience does your company have in the beauty industry? What numbers can I compare to what we're already doing now?"

Rose's mouth opened and then closed, a bewildered look on her face. "Honestly, you would be our first beauty company." She paused a moment, as if regrouping, and then sat forward, placing a folder on Juliette's desk. "These are the terms my boss has agreed to offer you when you come on board with us."

Opening the folder, Juliette glanced at the numbers, not impressed by them. She stared at Rose for several seconds before asking, "May I ask who your boss is?"

"Tristan Delacroix."

The guy with his face plastered on billboards and flyers throughout the city. Lifting the folder, she handed it back to Rose, who stared at it as if this had never happened to her before. "I appreciate you coming here and giving me the information, but I hired someone to work on marketing only a few months ago, and we're doing quite well when it comes to sales."

Rose took the folder. "I've pitched to several beauty companies recently, as that market is Tristan's main focus right now. Do you mind me asking what would entice you to hire a marketing company?"

Juliette sat back in her chair, seeing the woman in a new light. She wasn't just a minion sent out to land contracts; she was looking for a way to improve. After years of working and studying and reading everything she could on building a business, Juliette knew what it was like to hit a brick wall and have to ask for feedback to get past it.

Smiling at the woman, she said, "Honestly, some actual ideas of how you would market to our company. What would you do differently from what we do now? I'm sure there was a lot of work put into the information in that folder, but it all appeals to males. With skin care, we're focused on women, meaning what works for men has a higher chance of flopping with women. Information on studies you've researched from what other companies have done. Any of that would help me give it more thought."

Rose stood and nodded. "I appreciate that. I've tried to tell my boss that we need a different approach, but I like my job, and I don't want to lose it if I push the issue."

Juliette threw back her head and laughed. "What? He won't listen to you about a woman's industry when you're a woman? That doesn't surprise me."

"Do you know Mr. Delacroix?"

Shaking her head, Juliette said, "No, but when I can't turn without seeing his face plastered onto something, I know he's probably thinking he owns the world and nothing should change."

Rose grinned, nodding. "You're more right about that than I want to admit. Thank you for your time."

Juliette waited a few minutes before taking her purse out of her desk and heading out. "I'll be back in a few hours, Rachelle. I have my phone, so notify me if any emergencies happen."

Rachelle nodded. "I'll do that."

Walking out the doors, she turned to the left and walked toward the nearest subway entrance. As she descended the stairs, a billboard hung above. A picture of a man with dark brown hair, strong cheekbones, and a five o'clock shadow stared back at her.

Tristan Delacroix. Case in point. She really couldn't go anywhere without his face staring.

Blowing out a breath, she let the frustration go, grateful she wouldn't have to meet him, let alone work with him anytime soon.

To keep reading, check out *The French Billionaire.*

ALSO BY BRITNEY M MILLS

Love Austen Series

Love, Austen

Austen, Party of Two

Austen Unscripted

Matched, Austen

International Billionaire Club

The Australian Billionaire

The French Billionaire

The British Billionaire

The Vegas Billionaire

The Italian Billionaire

Christmas at Coldwater Creek

Love Locked

Love Lights

Love Shots

Subscribe to the newsletter to get updates on books coming out, cover reveals and the opportunity for giveaways!

ABOUT THE AUTHOR

Britney Mills was born in Utah but parts of her heart lie in Boston, Washington D.C. and Germany. Her love of writing began with the third grade book her teacher assigned her to write and she spent hours hidden behind her mother's couch writing pages and pages about knights and castles. Now she writes about romance. Go figure.

When she's not mothering her four small children, writing or reading, she's probably out playing a sport, going on a hike, or binge watching a murder mystery series. The way to her heart is through homemade chocolate chip cookies and five minutes peace.

ACKNOWLEDGMENTS

Thank you so much for reading this book! I hope you enjoyed it and make sure to leave a review!

You, the reader, are the one I think about as I work through these novels and thank you for continuing to support me. Starting a new series gets a little scary because it's new and I just hope you love these characters as much as I have.

To Annette, my new friend from Australia, for all you did to help me get the details in this book right. I learned so much about that great country and can't wait for the day when I can visit!

My husband deserves a lot of credit here as he takes care of life while I get these books ready to be published. Thank you, Max, for believing in me and for helping me realize my other dream.

Julie L. Spencer, Elizabeth McCay, Shannon Symonds and Deborah Goodman. Some of the best and funnest romance people I could associate with. I love our Thursday night chats and the late hours talking about whatever is going on in our lives. The long Facebook threads and the fun laughter as we work through our bad first drafts down to the final edits.

To Christina Schrunk for her patience in working with me on

these books. Her ideas and insight help to spark those last final puzzle pieces to help the book come together and I am so grateful for her.

To Krista Burdine for proofreading this book. She keeps me sane so I don't have to reread the book 100 times before publishing to hopefully get all of the errors out.

To Blue Valley Author Services, AKA Victorine Lieske and her awesome sister for making the cover. Especially for the last minute change of the guys eyes.

If you want news on when the next book comes out or my progress on the series, make sure to subscribe to the list so you don't miss anything.

We are grateful for readers like you and can't wait for you to enjoy the next book!